Also by M.L. Bullock

Desert Queen Saga
The Tale of Nefret
The Falcon Rises
The Kingdom of Nefertiti
The Song of the Bee Eater

Gulf Coast Paranormal Trilogy Series
Ghosted
Haunted
Dead
Spooked
Paranormal

Haunting Passions
Her Haunted Heart

Scary Fall Stories
Horrible Little Things

Seven Sisters
Seven Sisters
Ghost on a Swing

Twelve to Midnight
Mary Twelves
Pieces of Twelves

Standalone
Christmas at Seven Sisters
Delivered Me From Evil

Watch for more at www.mlbullock.com.

THE SONG OF THE BEE-EATER

By M.L. Bullock

I dedicate this book to sisters everywhere.
To make peace with your sister is to make peace with your own soul.

Table of Contents

Sung by his Harpist for Osiris, Chief of the Crew in the place of Truth

Inherkhawy, who says:

He is Happy this good prince:

Death is a kindly fate.

A Generation passes, Another stays,

Since the time of the ancestors.

The gods who were before rest in their tombs,

Blessed nobles too are buried in their tombs.

(Yet) those who built tombs,

Their places are gone,

What has become of them?

I have heard the words of Imhotep and Hordjedef,

Whose sayings are recited in whole.

What of their places?

Their walls have crumbled,

Their places are gone,

As though they had never been!

None comes from there,

To tell of their needs,

To calm our hearts,

Until we go where they have gone!

Hence rejoice in your heart!

Forgetfulness profits you,

Follow your heart as long as you live!

Put myrrh on your head,

Dress in fine linen,

Anoint yourself with oils fit for a god,

Heap up your joys,

Let your heart not sink!

Follow your heart and your happiness,

Do your things on earth as your heart commands!

When there comes to you that day of mourning,

the Weary-hearted (Osiris) hears not their mourning,

Wailing saves no man from the pit!

Make holiday, Do not weary of it!

Lo, none is allowed to take his goods with him,

Lo, none who departs comes back again!

The Harper's Song

(From the tomb walls of the priest Neferhotep)

1350 BC

Chapter One

Destiny's Daughter—Pah

I walked through the Oasis of Timia last night. A heavy purple sky draped over the encampment. No moon rose, but clear, bright stars pierced the veil above, allowing the glory of the Otherworld to shower down upon the camp below. The light of the heavens filtered through the tiny pinpricks left by the warring constellations of Sah and Sepdet. It bothered me that I could no longer recall the names I'd once called those constellations. Those Meshwesh names now escaped me—but I once had known all their names and could track their movements better than even the Old One, Farrah.

The soft slapping of the palm fronds grew louder on the evening desert breeze, and the chirping of night birds hungry for tasty moths broke the stillness of the early evening. The fluttering gray insects were always attracted to the amber lights of the camp lanterns, and there were many here along the main pathway that led to the tents of the King and the Council.

I smelled pleasant spices, cinnamon, and cardamom, lingering evidence of a celebratory meal. Happy memories stirred within me, memories from a more innocent time. As always with the Meshwesh, these feasts would last through much of the night, yet I dared not intrude. For although Timia had been home to me, I felt I was an intruder.

But why?

The memory of something seething and dark, complicated, and soul-shattering escaped me even though I reached for it, mentally clawed at it like one of the moths seeking the light that would burn its life away.

Forget, sister. Lest it kill you.

"Nefret?" I whispered into the night air. Her voice was in my ears, but I could not discern her tall, slender frame anywhere. I heard nothing else from her, and I poised hesitantly on the empty camp pathway, hoping no one would find me and cast me out. Now that I had returned home, I never wanted to leave again. Could it be possible that somehow I had returned? Perhaps so! I had never recovered the memory of my journey from Zerzura to Thebes. Couldn't I just as well have traveled home the same way?

The gods will have their way, won't they? They do as they please with us, I thought wryly.

I could see that I wore no royal robes this evening. Only a simple linen tunic of pale-yellow fabric. The soft grass beneath my bare feet was softer than any carpet I had ever trod upon. Tiny curls prickled on the back of my neck, rising in acknowledgment of the mystical realm that worked its magic here. Yes, indeed! As a worker of magic myself, I recognized the stickiness of the air, the shimmering movement of the invisible. Instinctively I touched the air around me, as I always did when I looked into the fire and the water. Then I noticed my hands. They were young again—the scars, and I had many, had been washed away by the magic and starlight, and I felt lighter than I had in many years.

Oh, how I have long staggered under the weight of my priestess' robes and the ornate jewels of Isis! Have I truly been set free?

Freedom overwhelmed me, and like a child, I spun in a joyful dance and laughed aloud. The sound was music to my own ears. How long had it been since I laughed or felt peace like this?

The whistling songs of my people, the Meshwesh, floated toward me and tugged at my heartstrings. Yes, I had been correct! A celebration was underway, and I could hear the excitement rising in their voices. From the pitch and tune, I knew what this was—a birth waiting, a holy night for us. I heard the clapping of hands as the expectant mother settled into her tent. How happy they were! Yes, a child would come! A child for the tribe—a treasure.

Treasure? What have I forgotten?

The wind rose again, and the bright blue pennants above my father's tent beckoned to me. Yes, that was where I should go. He would welcome me, make them understand that I was a true Meshwesh daughter. I was also a treasure, and I belonged to them. He would put his robes on me and grant me whatever I wished. *Father! I come to you!*

"Hold now, daughter of Isis. What are you doing here?"

Blinking into the dim light, I whispered, "Who is there?" A figure hovered at the corner of the tent. It was a woman. She was not tall as Farrah yet carried herself like one with authority. At my question she stepped onto the lighted path, and I caught my breath.

It was Mina! Mina, who was not dead but young again, her raven's-wing hair hanging freely down her back. And she spoke! Instinctively I made the sign of respect, but she did not return the gesture. This troubled me.

"What of your vow, Mina?" I felt compelled to ask. While yet a girl, the acolyte had taken a vow of silence. I had heard her speak only a handful of times in my life, and then only in ritual service to the tribe. By her speaking so plainly, I knew that deep magic indeed worked here in this place this night. She said nothing for a long moment. Her hair fluttered like the pennants of Father's tent, covering her dark eyes from my view. I felt the power of those eyes as they searched my soul. I did not fight her or argue my case. I could not remember my offenses, so why should she? I only wanted to belong to my people again. To be their treasure once more.

"I ask you again, why have you come, daughter of Isis?"

"I am a daughter of the Red Lands!" I protested the repeated accusation. "You know me, Mina. It is I, Pah hap Semkah!"

My answer did not move her, and finally, the wind lifted her hair away from her tanned face. I could see her liquid brown eyes, and I relaxed under their sympathetic consideration. Her eyes did not condemn me. I saw only sadness there. "Look above you, then, and tell me what you see," she commanded, raising her right hand. Gazing upward I immediately recognized the constellation—it was Osiris with his bow. It was a dark omen indeed.

"I see Osiris, Mina. He faces the west now." Hoping to impress her, I added, "And look! A star falls like an arrow from his bow!"

"He is known as the Dancing Man to the Meshwesh. Or have you forgotten all our ways, Pah hap Semkah?"

"I-I know what is important. I know I should be here." Desperation rose in my voice.

Mina inched toward me, her eyes like fire, her voice like steel. "Remember, Pah. Remember your promise to her."

I stepped away from her. "No! I don't want to remember." I raised my hand upward as if she would strike me. "I want to stay here with my father and my people!"

"You want what you cannot have, but that has always been your way. You will keep your promise to her."

Although her words·stung my heart, I knew she spoke the truth. I begrudgingly nodded and pleaded, "Let me pass, Mina. Let me go to my father just once more."

Like a wraith, she vanished into smoke, and I was alone again. The distance to Father's tent was only a few feet, but it might as well have been a mile. I could not will my feet to make that journey. I desperately hoped Mina was wrong, but I knew she wasn't.

I have left something undone. Something important.

A shadow passed beside me, and I spun to catch sight of who came near me. There was no one there, only whispers in the dark.

"Mina?" I whispered back to the empty air. The shadow whirred by me again, and this time it pinched me. I gasped and felt increasingly alarmed. This was not Mina but some other being that did not want me here.

With a quick, wistful glance toward Father's tent, I began to run toward the pool. Yes. I would find peace there. Maybe a place to hide from this shadow and whatever promise I had made that might prevent me from coming home! A gray moth flapped in front of me, leading me down the now sandy path, and I took it as a sign. Quietly and quickly, I closed the distance between myself and the water. I could smell the water now. At last, I would taste the waters of Timia one more time!

As I cleared the last of the tents, I glanced around me but saw no one lingering. There were no more tents, no place for shadows to hide. All the Meshwesh were at the celebration on the other side of the expansive camp.

All except Alexio, who stood waiting with his back against the tallest palm tree. My mind whispered, "This must be a dream." My heart replied, "No! This is real. Let it be real!"

His arms were crossed lazily, and his dark hair hung around his shoulders. His expressive almond-shaped eyes watched me approach, and that thrilled my soul. He watched me as a man would watch a woman he desired, and that was all I had ever wanted. To have his love, to own his heart, and to share my own with him.

"Alexio? Can it be you? What are you doing here?"

"I came to see you, little dove."

"I have not heard you call me that in such a long time. You came for *me*? Truly?" I dared not hope that his words were true. Alexio often toyed with my heart, and I always let him. It was exquisite torture.

Again, the memory of a great wrong threatened to encroach upon this happy moment, and again, I willed it away. The mental struggle made me feel weak, and I had the growing sense that I would not be able to prevent its reappearance for long. "How long have you waited, Alexio?" I wanted to hear his warm, melodious voice a little longer.

In the distance, a lone musician plucked skillfully at the strings of his rebab, and the notes plucked at my heart. Alexio was only a few feet away now. I could see the angled curve of his high cheekbones and smell the cedar oil on his skin. His dark eyes were almost the deepest purple, so brown were they. He did not mock me as he used to do. He did not tease with his eyes. This was the culmination of all my life's desire, to be loved by Alexio and to show him love. I had cast everything aside—yes, even my own sister, Nefret—in an attempt to capture his heart. I loved him with a ferocity few could understand.

"I want to stay here, Alexio. Promise me I can stay with you. Now and forever." I reached for him. My hand shook as it approached his face. He gazed down at me, his eyes half-closed, a sad smile on his face. Just one touch. To know I was real and he was real, and we were alive and home.

"Pah!" Mina's voice called from behind me, the warning tone freezing me in mid-motion. My hand was so close to Alexio's face that I could feel the warmth of his skin. "Would you leave with a promise broken? You cannot return here if you do."

I did not want to turn around and see her there. I wanted to forget the horrible things, the promise, the shadow. Alexio's sorrowful eyes were fixed upon mine and mine upon his.

"Alexio?"

"Do what you must, little dove. I will be here." His look was serious, and he cast his gaze at Mina behind me. Still, I would not look away.

"Tell me just once," I whispered to him as I lowered my hand.

"Pah! Come away!" Mina's rough voice warned me. I dared not ignore her for much longer.

Only a second more. This is life. This is my everything.

He bent his head down as if to kiss me, but as our lips came together, the shadow that dogged my steps earlier zipped between us, and he vanished.

"No! Alexio!" I screamed and clung to the trunk of the tree, sobbing in despair.

Mina's hand rested on my shoulder now. I bent under the weight of it, and although her touch was light, it brought the heaviness of the memories I had hoped to avoid. "Daughter of Isis, Daughter of the Red Lands, Daughter of Destiny. Do what you must do—keep your promise. Now is the time. A life for a life."

Her words launched me through the grass of the oasis. I passed unseen by my clan as they awaited the arrival of another treasure. Helplessly I shot through the Red Lands nearly as quickly as the star that had fallen from Osiris' bow. With another breath, I flew through the pylons of the outer gate and the massive green-gold doors of the Green Temple of Isis. I flew up and up, until once again, I was in my room. My acolyte Shepshet did not so much as stir or blink an eyelash, but I bolted upright in my bed in time to see the supernatural wind that had carried me there extinguish all the lights in my room.

That had been no dream. I had been to the Otherworld! Like Mina, who died many years ago, Alexio was dead too. I could not join them because I still had life in my body, but it was a doomed life and would soon end.

The growing perception that there was another presence here with us rose within me. "I know you are here. Come out and show yourself," I said bravely, but all my courage rose from the bitterness that threatened once again to overwhelm me.

"High One? Do you call me? What has happened to the light?"

"Silent, Shepshet. The dead are here. Close your eyes and do not open them until I tell you, lest they take you with them when they leave."

"Yes, lady," she whimpered, burying her face in her covers. I could hear the rustling of cloth, and I examined the darkness, waiting for her to appear. Cold crept into my bones, but I did not move a muscle.

"You have what you want. I have given him up, Paimu. Again! I have given him up. Take my life if you must, but do it now! Do not torment me forever!"

Then she stepped out of the shadows of the open window near my balcony. Paimu, the girl I'd murdered fifteen seasons ago. In the moonlight of this world, I could see her clearly. Thankfully she did not have bloodless skin, black eyes, and bloodstained clothing, as she often had when she appeared to me over the years. It was as if I were looking at a true human girl. The vision broke my heart.

"Paimu! Is it time now? Do you demand my life this night? I am ready to go. Ready to return to Timia."

She refused to answer but walked to the balcony, I noticed that she wore the white sandals my sister had given her before her death. Surely that meant something. She gazed toward the west, toward the sprawling desert beyond Pharaoh's massive city Akhetetan, or Amarna as some had begun to call it. To my eyes, it was a golden prison. Nothing more.

I remained in the doorway for fear that she would push me over the side of the balcony. From this great height at the top of the Green Temple of Isis, there would be no doubt I would die instantly in such a fall. In fact, Nakmaa, the old priestess before me, had left this realm in such a manner. There had been talk of murder, but no one could prove it.

Paimu's fixed gaze compelled me to overcome my fear. I stepped out behind her, and in that instant, a big blue ball of flame passed overhead. Like the star that fell in my dream—or was it a vision?—this star also fell from Osiris' bow. "What now?"

Paimu pointed west, where the star fell. West to Zerzura.

"Zerzura! I must warn the queen!"

Paimu turned slowly, and now her back was against the railing. She was so close that, if she had been alive, I could have pushed her over.

No! Do not think such evil thoughts, Pah! She is but a child, and you have killed her once already!

My face flushed, and I asked her, "Why have you come, child? I know I owe you a life. Do you want me to cut my wrists? Am I to jump from here?" Paimu stared at me and gave me no answer. "What is it?" I screamed at her. Shepshet muffled a scream from her pallet next to my bed.

A loud boom reverberated through the temple, and another fallen star illuminated the city below. I wasn't the only one to have seen it. I could hear the people below scream in confusion and fear.

Gliding toward me quickly, Paimu stood a few inches from my face. I could see luminous tears in her eyes as if she lived!

"What? What is it, Paimu?"

"Nefff—rettt…" she whispered fearfully and then vanished into wisps of smoke. Soon her presence was gone, and the room began to warm. Awareness and understanding came over me like a great wave. Oh, yes, it was time.

"Shepshet! Get up! We must prepare to see Pharaoh! He will send for us soon!"

"What? How do you know, lady?" She pulled the cloth off her head and ran to me on the balcony. "Who is Paimu?"

"Please! No questions, for we haven't much time."

She screamed as another star fell on Amarna, and I prepared for what was to come. Pharaoh would want to hear from his many advisers, including the High Priestess of the Green Temple of Isis. As I allowed Shepshet and the others to dress my hair and my body, I wondered exactly what I would tell him.

Whatever it would be, my true mission was clear. Protect my sister. The debt would be collected.

A life for a life.

Chapter Two

Priestess of Isis—Pah

As I rose from the chair, the stiff robe hung heavily from my shoulders. My eyes were lined with gold, and Shepshet had pressed shiny powder all over my face and hands. Staring at myself in the ornate mirror, a gift from Nefret, I thought I looked very much like a being from another realm. *Good. This will play nicely.* Just as I had anticipated, Pharaoh's steward came to collect me. I was ready to leave the solace of my rooms and temple for his court. It was a strange thing for a high priestess to leave the temple for any occasion, except for the birth blessing of Pharaoh's new children or some other royal ceremony.

I walked down the long stairway. Dozens of my acolytes were sitting on the steps, watching my every move. I did not rush myself, and I did not miss a step. I did not look at any of their faces, but I could sense their fear. Even the most ignorant priestess would know these falling stars were not omens of prosperity for the kingdom. As I arrived at the final step, I stopped and spoke to one of the acolytes. "I see fear on your face, priestess. What is your name?"

"Yuyu, lady."

"When I return, Yuyu, I hope to see calm and serenity reflected in those eyes. Go now to the water and stay there until you have defeated your fear. Ask the goddess to send you a vision to make you whole again." It might have been wrong to single her out, but sometimes making an example of one gave benefits to many. It was for the greater good.

Shamefaced, she bent her head and bowed before me.

The heavy doors were opened now, the ones I'd flown through earlier. I stepped outside, and the steward led me to the litter that waited for me. "No, I will not travel that way. I want to walk."

"I beg your pardon, High One, but Pharaoh insists that you come quickly. With the streets so congested now, it would take an hour or more to reach him on foot. I cannot allow that. Please come with me."

I gave him a surly look but obeyed. Whatever he might say, I would walk back. I longed to see the city streets for myself at least once more. It had been so long since I had walked anywhere outside the complex. I had not previously had the courage to walk through the doors except for on official duties. Tonight's display of falling skies had broken that fear. Paimu would not murder me herself. I would soon lay myself on the altar. For many years I feared her ghost would kill me as soon as I stepped outside the protection of the goddess. I was about to die anyway, and my death would be for a purpose.

And then we will be even, Paimu.

The steward did not speak to me about the celestial event or anything else as we rode double-time to the Golden Palace. It was once called the Palace of the Happy Sovereigns, in the first years after its building, but that name was not used anymore. Now the palace was an unhappy place with too many wives, too much intrigue, and a spirit of greed and opulence that touched all who entered it. As the litter came to a stop and the brightly painted box I sat on touched the ground, the steward slipped out and drew back the curtains to make room for my exit. To my surprise, I had been led not to the entrance of the throne room where these meetings typically took place but to the lower gardens, a private place I knew my sister used. It was her sanctuary.

"High One, the Great Queen would have audience with you before you join the other mage in the Sky Room."

"Oh, I see," I said, acting as bored as I could. "I hope this doesn't take too long. I am sure Pharaoh is anxious to see me," I lied as I smoothed my gowns neatly. I had no love for Amenhotep. I had admired him long ago, but I'd long since lost respect for him. Too much had happened between him and my sister. He shamed her by bringing his harem into the palace. He was no honorable man.

"Yes, but the Great Queen insists. Please." The steward, a new royal whose name I could not remember, bowed as he opened the small blue door that led to the garden. At least Nefret still held her title. That was something to be thankful for.

"Very well, but do not leave here. I will be inside only a few minutes. I cannot tarry," I told him.

"Yes, lady," he answered none the wiser. Over the years, many rumors had circulated about Nefret and me. That we hated one another, that we weren't truly sisters. And even more notorious rumors that I wouldn't entertain. None of them were true. We did not hate one another. Although I rarely saw her or heard from her, we were not enemies as we once had been. That she would want to see me privately, especially on such an evening, was a rare thing.

I walked silently down the path, my eyes adjusting quickly to the darkness. Vines and shrubs were carefully sculpted into twisted works of art in my sister's garden. They looked like living things, mystical creatures in the low light of the moonless night sky. I'd been here a few years ago at the coming home of Nefret's first daughter, Meritaten. I had not been invited back, although I could not recall the reason why.

In the daylight hours, the cheerfully painted walls told the story of a happy family. The white stone walls were painted with images of the royal couple and their family worshiping the Aten, sailing across the lake, offering the lotus and fruits to their favorite deity. One especially touching portrait showed Amenhotep and Nefret playing with their children, but now the images stayed in the shadows. I shivered at the thought. These were sweet pictures of the way things had once been. They were not that way now.

Even though I did not dwell in the palace, I had heard the gossip about my sister and Aperel. Lies. All of them. No one loved Amenhotep more than Nefret, and she would never put her children at risk by flitting about with Pharaoh's horse master. I knew this because I knew what she'd already sacrificed.

The Great Queen was threatened constantly on all sides. She would be cast down from her lofty position, replaced by Tadukhipa or the concubine, Ipy. I did not believe it, but I did not envy my sister. Managing such a tangled web took talent—a talent I did not have.

As I approached the inner garden, trepidation crept up my spine. I heard nothing, not even her voice. Then I saw her. Nefret squatted on the ground, looking at something, and I stood quietly in the archway of the garden, waiting for her to notice me. Even though I was her sister, I could not barge into her presence without being welcomed. Protocol was everything, and we had to keep up all appearances. Especially now when it mattered the most.

Finally, she stood, with whatever it was she examined in her shaking hands. Nefret's red hair hung unbrushed down her back in clumps. She wore a lavender gown that showed the rounded shape of her body and an unbound belt of gold rope. Her clothing was in the Grecian style, a style my sister favored lately, I'd been told.

"Sister, look! Look what they have done!" She held the bundle out toward me.

"What is that? A bird?" Forgetting formality after seeing no one joined us, I did as she asked. I took the bird and examined it. It was no ordinary bird—this was a falcon. Nothing was amiss except its head lolled pitifully as if someone had snapped its neck.

"Who would make such an open threat?"

"I do not know. It was left here where I could find it. I cannot think who would commit such a heinous act."

Who indeed? I thought. The list was endless. The priests of Amun hated Nefret and her husband. Dozens of concubines and a handful of sister-wives also rose up my mental list of potential evildoers. "For now, let's put that question aside and ask another one. Why would they do such a thing? I think the answer is clear, my queen."

"Tell me, then, Pah. I must know. The sight of this fills me with dread. I've seen dead animals before, but this..."

How much to tell her? I couldn't gauge her mind. I sized her up carefully, trying to determine what to share with her. Her makeup was streaked as if she'd been crying, and not over a dead falcon. Nefret's waist was thicker than it used to be, but that was to be expected after producing six children in fast succession. I hated that Amenhotep treated her like a broodmare.

"You came to the throne as the Desert Queen, the Falcon of the Red Lands. Someone is warning you that your time is coming to an end." Nefret gasped and put her hand to her chest. "Surely that hasn't escaped you, sister."

"Can you look for me? Look in the fire and the water, Pah. Tell me who it is! Who will kill me, sister?"

I put the bird into a nest of heart-shaped leaves and pulled Nefret next to me on a nearby bench. My heart broke for her, and I also felt dread rising in me. How strange that my twin and I would still be tied together even after all that had passed between us. I said in a low, stern whisper, "Listen and don't speak." I glanced around me before proceeding. "You must leave, Nefret. I will grant you asylum in the Green Temple of Isis. You cannot stay in Amarna. Disaster is coming here...and to Zerzura. Neither place will be safe. The stars have fallen from the bow of Osiris, the Dancing Man! It is a sure sign of disaster to this kingdom and all those living in its shadow."

"What? I cannot leave my husband and my kingdom, Pah! I can't run away because of a dead bird and a few falling stars. Surely you make too much of this. Is this some kind of trick?" She was on her feet now, anger flashing in her eyes.

"Sister, my sister." I rose, taking her hand. "We are beyond this distrust, aren't we? Haven't I faithfully served you all these years?" For a long moment, we stared at one another. When she didn't argue, I continued, "You know that I love you above all others, but the time to complete things has come. Paimu came to me again. It is my time, a life for a life, and she will have it no other way. I will die. But you must live, sister. You must live for your children. Smenkhkare, Tasherit, and Meritaten, they must live! They are our treasures." I clasped her hands. Tears threatened to flood my eyes, but I held them back. I needed to keep a calm demeanor if I was to face Pharaoh with any degree of authority.

"But Seritaten...all my babies."

"I know you mourn for them, but those children are dead, and you cannot take them with you. You must think reasonably. Think of the ones who live still." I could hear the gate opening behind me, and I stepped back from her. "I have to go to Pharaoh now, Great Queen." In a whisper I added, "I will make him believe that all is well, but I tell him this only for your benefit. Listen to me now. We don't have much time."

"Are you sure, Pah? I can't bear to hear you speak like this. Surely you are wrong. And what about Father?"

I glanced over her shoulder, thinking that I saw someone move in the darkness, but there was no one. "What Farrah said about him, that he will die for love, will come true. In this, she was right. But you cannot think about him right now. You must do the practical things to prepare. When you receive the sign from me, you must leave with all haste. No dallying or all will be for naught. And you must cut your hair. Shave it."

"What?" She reached for her tangled hair, her eyes wide with surprise.

"Do you want to live? Or am I wasting my time?"

"I care nothing for my life anymore, but I want my children to live, Pah," she said, swallowing hard.

"No questions, then, and let no one see you do this. You cannot have your servants help you. Burn the hair so no one finds it. Keep your head covered so no one sees."

Nefret was crying softly now, but she didn't argue with me. Time was growing short, and Pharaoh's servants lingered inside the door of the garden. As if his servants and hers worked together, her servants also appeared and hung near her now. She yelled at them, "Go away, Menmet. I am fine." To me, she said, "What do you have planned? Can you not tell Akhenaten the truth? Is he in danger?"

"We are all in danger, sister! It is not human hands at work here. Listen and obey, please. I have never asked anything from you since I've been here, but I ask now. Do as I ask so I can help you. All will be made clear. Look for a sign, Nefret, if you do not believe me." I felt the magic prickle in my throat. "Yes, a sign you will know. And when that happens, do not question me, but obey."

Nefret wrapped her arms around me. "I will do as you ask, only don't leave me, Pah. My own sister, my heart, and my treasure!"

She sobbed now, and my heart was not a stone. I wanted to take her hand and run away with her, back to our home at Timia, but there were others to consider. Smenkhkare, Meritaten, Tasherit, and yes, even Kames.

"One last thing. Trust no one. You must look to the Grecians, our mother's people, for help. There is one who will help you. His name is Adijah. He will know what to do."

"I have done this to us, haven't I? My ambition. My love for Akhenaten."

"Nonsense. If there is anyone to blame, it is me. It was you who should have been mekhma. You would have led us to Zerzura, but we cannot think about those long-ago things now. Even our home is in danger. Enough with the past! Think of the future! Don't forget, look for the sign. I will make sure Adijah comes to you soon."

"Will I see you again?"

There was no fire and water to peer into, but somehow I knew the answer to that question. "Yes, you will see me once more. I must go, sister. Pharaoh waits." Without waiting for her to stop crying, I walked out of the garden and followed the waiting steward.

Time for lies. And soon it would be time to die.

Chapter Three

Mines of Blood—Semkah

From the rocks above, I saw the rebels murder my messenger. They slid a sword down his throat as he screamed and left him pinned to the ground with their blades. I swallowed the bile that rose up within me. I felt Zubal's breath draw quickly beside me and then release angrily, yet he did not put words to what he witnessed. For that I was thankful.

Now that the rebels had claimed the mine, it appeared they had no intention of quickly robbing and relinquishing the property as I had hoped. The mine's secret location had been found, and the nearby tribes—even faraway tribes like the Algat and Kuni—would come in search of it now without fear. I prayed that Omel's hand was not upon this. I could not believe that it was. It was a miracle that the location had been kept secret this long, but no more. I had no doubt that whoever these men claimed to be, they were here by consent of Egypt's greedy Pharaoh, my son-in-law. In the past few months, he'd demanded more gold than ever before, much more than we could supply him without killing those who dug for the treasures. I feared that our mines' resources would soon be exhausted as the turquoise mine had been. He had seen to that. He would not seize it for himself directly, the two-faced bastard. Not out in the open. That would break my treaty with him. Instead, he sent robbers to steal from me and pretended he knew nothing about it, all the time demanding more gold. His gold! I spat at the idea. It was Meshwesh gold!

I had not wanted to draw my daughter into our negotiations, if you could call them that, but her husband's gold lust made her involvement a necessity. If I did not succeed here today, I had no other choice. She must help us. Omel had not been successful in shielding us from Egyptian greed. I had warned him of this all those years ago.

"Are those truly Meshwesh, king? Why would they betray us? How could they do such evil?"

"Egypt corrupts everything. That blade is not ours. These odious men were bought with a price, Zubal. We are not safe. Not even behind the walls of Zerzura. These men," I said as I pointed toward the mine, "are no longer Meshwesh but traitors. To kill my messenger, their own brother, is to defy our ancestors and the gods—and me! Now they will pay the price for such blasphemy. Are you ready, Zubal? We will burn the entrance. Seal it up and leave them to their doom."

"Yes, Semkah! We stand ready with the carts and all that you have ordered."

"Call the archers. Line them here, and here." I squatted and drew in the sand, unwilling to reveal my hand to the criminals below. I wanted them to be surprised. "At my command, begin firing. They'll retreat, cowards that they are, at least for a few minutes. During that time, you and the others fill the entrance with everything you can find, anything that burns. We will show them how we treat robbers and murderers."

Zubal nodded grimly, and I gave the shrill whistle that signaled our advance. We couldn't take the mine back without destroying some part of it. They had food and water enough to last for weeks, but time wasn't on our side. Pharaoh expected his gold, and if I could not deliver, he would rain down fire upon us. But I would show him I was no small king, no weak man.

"Run! Now!" When Zubal's men were in place, I whistled again and began making my way down the steep wall myself. It was no easy task with only one arm to steady me, but I did not dare slow down. The blue and green arrows of my archers began to fly through the air toward the front of the mine. As expected, the cowards sought refuge inside, but a few made attempts to return fire. Luckily for us, they were better thieves than warriors. In just a few minutes, Zubal and his men had covered half the front of the mine with the carts and every bit of rubbish they could find. They placed the small keg in the center at the base. The trapped men jeered at Zubal and his men but then sensed that something was seriously wrong and began to plead for their lives.

I considered the plea for as long as it took me to see Alora's body dragged back to my camp. He had been a faithful servant of Leela's. She'd insisted he come to protect me, but now the old man was dead. Now I had to tell my wife the bad news, that her cousin gave his life obeying my command.

Zubal nocked an arrow, a red one signifying my royal vengeance. We stood side by side now, fifty feet from the entrance. I yelled at the rebels, "You have done evil here. You have taken what was not yours. You have killed your brother. You will die."

To my surprise, I saw one round face appear. He wore a mocking grin, but his voice was not as confident as he pretended to be. "What? You're going to kill ten of us with one arrow? Come any closer, and we'll do more than hurl sticks at you, one-armed king. Go away, old man. Leave this work to the younger men. We have swords, and these rickety carts won't stop us from finishing you off."

"What is your name?" Zubal shouted. He relaxed his grip for a moment and waited.

"You don't remember me? I am Hadja, the son of Garimer. He died in these mines, gave his life to them. Your bastard king sent him here. Now this place belongs to me. I paid for it with my father's blood, as did all these men here with me."

I ignored his accusation. I did not use slaves in my mines. Free men who were freely paid worked here. If he supposed something else, I had no obligation to tell him differently. I had no sympathy for Hadja and his father.

I signaled to Zubal to raise the bow and arrow once more and said, "You are so like your father, Hadja, but at least he accepted his punishment like a man although he was a coward through and through. Why do you think he came here? He abandoned his people when the Kiffians rode through Timia. He begged to earn back his honor, and thus he was given the chance to work in the mine. And he would still be working this day if he had not stolen from us. But enough talk. You are not worth even the cost of a few words."

Hadja railed at me, but I did not entertain him further. Zubal and I walked back a few steps, and then I gave the order. "Now, Zubal."

The young man released the arrow, and it shot fiercely from his white bow and landed in the keg we'd placed at the center of the mine. The men behind the carts began to laugh and mock us. They didn't appear to see the green liquid seep from the wooden cask, not until Zubal nocked the fiery arrow.

Zubal shot the second arrow, and as expected, it landed in the cask. We saw the flash of light and began to run to the mouth of the canyon opening. We had only a few seconds. Diving for cover, Zubal threw himself on top of me as the ground shook and the mine's entrance collapsed in a pile of rubble, dust, and sand. No sound issued from the rocky chamber, and there were no further pleas for mercy. There was nothing at all.

My men gathered our supplies, and we somberly trekked back to the camp. None of us wanted to discuss what had happened. Our brothers had betrayed us, as Egypt had betrayed us, and we had destroyed our only remaining source of income. I wasn't sure they realized the danger of what we'd done. We would have to abandon the White City. Egypt would come for us. There was no doubting that. Still, for the moment at least, we had victory. I slapped Zubal's shoulder and nodded respectfully at him. "Hironus himself never shot a truer arrow. Thank you, my friend."

"I am grateful for the accuracy, but it is an evil thing to kill another brother. There are so few of us now."

I understood that feeling and respected him for it. "Well, at least there is one fewer coward. You were not wrong to have killed him. Alora deserves vengeance."

He nodded and made the sign of respect. There were only twenty-four in our party. Thankfully, it had been enough to do the job.

Now it was done. Zerzura was two days' ride to the north, but we'd stay one night at Farya, the small oasis just north of the mine. We crested a dune, and immediately my heart sagged into my stomach. Our camp had been burned. The tents were gone, and there was nothing left but a few scorched poles and dead cattle. With a shout of anger, I spurred the camel on, with my men assembled behind me. Leela and a few other women had traveled with us, and now they were gone, taken by an unknown enemy. I screamed, and the other men wailed as they too saw the camp's destruction. Zubal and I immediately began looking for tracks. We didn't have to search far since the raiders hadn't bothered to hide them. Those who had taken our women were headed north to Zerzura.

"Why would they leave the cattle behind? This is not a raiding party." Zubal spat on the ground and eyeballed the vast stretch of sand that lay between us and home.

"No, it is not," I agreed glumly. "This is an act of war. We must ride! They can't be too far ahead of us. There are still flames from the fire."

My back ached, and a recent sore on my arm had flared. I could feel it bleeding but said nothing. My wife was at the mercy of bandits, likely Meshwesh bandits who'd betrayed us on Egypt's behalf. I had no doubt the "Heretic King," as he was called, was behind this. A strange wind blew across the sand, and we covered our faces with our head scarves for protection.

We rode hard for a few hours, following the tracks easily until we saw the first body. A blonde woman, the foreign wife of Zubal's son, lay nude and bloody in the sand. The sight sickened me but Thiel, Zubal's son, behaved honorably. He and his father wrapped the girl in Thiel's cloak and rolled her lifeless body down the dune, forever out of sight of the eyes of men. Thiel didn't hide his tears but wept silently. Zubal patted his shoulder, assuring him that she would have vengeance, and we returned to the trail. Not long after the first bloody find, we came across two more bodies, a man we did not know, and Kay, a Meshwesh wife. We assumed that the man was one of the bandits and had killed by Kay, judging by her heartbreaking wounds. Kay was wife to Amadaxes and a dear friend of my own wife.

"They think to slow us down with this murderous parade," Zubal replied quietly.

"And they have succeeded, but I will not deny these men the opportunity to bury their wives. Look at this man. See?" I pointed to his wrist tattoo. "I thought him to be a tribesman, but this proves he is no tribal thief. That is Egyptian script."

"Whether freeman or slave, he is no doubt Egyptian. And look there!"

Smoke billowed in the distance, and we raced back to our animals, eager to make for the scene. With each dune we crested, I pressed my dry lips together and prayed that I would not find Leela lying dead in the sand. Then we saw the camp sprawled before us. "Stop! Back and down!" I said to the men behind me. Sliding off the brute camel, I scrambled to the top of the dune on my belly. It had grown dark now. Only a few stars had appeared above us. The raiders didn't seem to notice or mind that we'd followed them. They were acting as if they had nothing to worry about. They were either brave or stupid—or this was a trap. I suspected the latter.

"What now?" Thiel said angrily. "I am eager for blood, my king. We should take them while it is dark."

"No. They will expect that."

"But what they've done! We may not have another chance!" Thiel did not approve of my answer, but he was smart enough not to reproach me.

"Thiel, can I trust you?"

"Always, my king. Always."

"Take one other man and ride to Zerzura. Tell Orba what has happened and bring back men. At dawn, we will ride down and take back what is ours, and you will have your blood cost. I promise you."

"But what they will endure tonight!" Thiel burst into angry tears. I did not chide him.

I gripped his shoulder. "My own wife is there, Thiel. I know you worry about your mother, but we do not have the men to save our women. We must keep watch tonight. It is the only way."

"It will be done," Zubal said for his son. Thiel's face was a contortion of agony, but he offered no further objections. He walked backward and made the sign of respect. I signed back and told Zubal, "It will be a long night. No fires, and tell the men to spread out. We must keep watch until our brothers join us."

"It will be done, Semkah." My friend paused and pointed at my tunic. "But do tend to your wound, or you'll bleed to death before the sun rises. Your wife will kill me if you die." I grinned at him, thinking of Leela's anger rising upon the brave Zubal. My wife was a fiery woman, not like Kadeema, who'd been all dreams and love and softness. When Kadeema disappeared, I thought she had taken all my love with her. But Leela brought love back to me, and her love was far greater than I deserved.

Now I had to show her how much I loved her. I lay with my back to the sand, staring up at the sky. I recounted the many times we'd lain together. The tender moments when she'd bathed me and cared for me after the loss of my arm. And she'd shown her love in greater ways than that. She cared for Pah in her madness and helped me lead my people into a time of peace, although it was short-lived.

Suddenly, a shrill scream ripped through the night. I could not tell who it was I heard, but I feared the worst.

Stay strong, my wife! Stay strong for me! Endure until the morning!

I refused to allow my mind to wander, to consider what might be done to her even at this moment. No doubt her strength and beauty would draw the attention of some evil man. And when they learned who she was, how much more would she suffer? Agony washed over me. I leaned back even harder into the sand, my short sword resting on my chest, when I heard another sound. A dull thud burst above us. I opened my eyes and sat up anxiously as the sky filled with bright blue light. A star fell and then another. They didn't stop falling.

"Look!" Zubal said, pointing below. The camp of men below us, at least seventy-five of them, had rushed out of their tents to watch the celestial display. Their confusion was obvious, and more than a dozen camels fled from the camp. "Perhaps the gods are on our side! We should go down, Semkah, and take them back now! This is a sign." The others gathered around him. There were fewer than twenty men now. Thiel and a few other warriors had left us to do my bidding. Another star fell, this one with a thunderous sound.

I couldn't deny this was a sign from above. Even the simplest among us would know that. Another star passed overhead, and it fell toward Egypt in a burst of white light. My heart sank for my daughters. I could not help them now. They had been beyond my reach for a very long time, but I had one daughter left. *Sumaway!* She was my daughter and Leela's, and she was at home in Zerzura. How could I face her if I let her mother die this night when I could have prevented it? This I had to do for her—and for me.

"Live or die, let us go down. What do you have in mind, Zubal?" I grinned at him, ready to give my life for Leela and the other Meshwesh women. Even if it meant my life, I would see her face one more time.

Chapter Four

The Third Mekhma—Orba

"Time to rise up, Orba. Come now. Don't make it difficult for me. You know I am not as strong as you. Sit up and drink, please."

Blinking into the brightness, I tried to obey Sumaway's request, but I felt feeble. My bones ached, and my muscles felt like taut skins pulled over a drum. With so much pain, I surely had to die soon. I welcomed such release. I did not know how much more pain I could bear without behaving like a lunatic. At first the pain came and went, but not anymore. The pain appeared one morning and never departed. It was like a fog that rolled in and tried to smother the life out of me. It had succeeded.

"Very well, you may use the straw. But you must at least lift your head, or you'll choke." She poked the straw into the drink and tapped the end of it, capturing the liquid. I opened my dry mouth and allowed her to drip the pain-killing potion in. She did this several times until I had enough of the liquid to affect me. The potion would not heal me, but I would not hurt as much. I felt the warmth of the juice filter through my body. The pain began to subside almost immediately but in a limited way. The truth was if the disease did not kill me, the painkiller eventually would. Either way, death wasn't far from me.

"I know you want to lie there and die, but you can't. My father needs you. He sent a messenger for you. The trouble at the mines has escalated, and my mother and the other women have been taken. Semkah needs you! Thiel is just outside the door, Orba. You have to see him."

Her pleading voice and her faith in me touched me, but my body had a difficult time obeying her command. After a few moments of struggle, Sumaway showed her natural impatience. "Are you even trying?"

I did not care for her tone, but I was in no position to school her on manners. Sumaway was not a patient young woman, not like her mother. She reminded me of her sisters in so many ways, but in the area of patience, she followed Pah's path, always ready to move forward without question or worry about the destruction it might create. I wished she had known them. I loved the girl like she was my own, but I could not do as she asked. My body would not allow my obedience. I let out a sad sigh.

"Now is the time for you to lead, Sumaway. You must guide the people in your father's stead. At least until he returns. I cannot." I could barely put the sentences together, but I knew she did not believe me. It was as if she believed I lay here on my sickbed because I wanted to, as if I wanted to die.

"You must try," she said as she fussed with my tunic and tried to force me up.

I gasped in pain. It shot through my bones like fire. "Stop fighting me. You cause me even more pain. Send in the messenger, girl."

I was tempted to close my eyes as she left me. I was on the edge now. The line between life and death blurred quickly. Yes, I could close my eyes and drift away from this world, but I did not. I had to stay here a little longer for Sumaway.

Thiel rushed in and bowed on his knee in the traditional manner of a messenger. "Old One, Semkah sends me to tell you what has happened." In a rush, the young man told the horrible story. The worst had happened. Egypt had all but seized the mine, and many of our brothers had betrayed us. To make matters worse, Leela and the women who had insisted on traveling with her were now at the mercy of those betrayers. Why had she gone with them? If anyone had bothered to ask me, I would have advised against it. I knew I must do something immediately, but my mind could not gather the proper thoughts. What should I say?

Sumaway stood by my side and dabbed my forehead with a linen cloth. She waited for me to speak. Thiel rose from his knees and towered above me. Sumaway spoke in low tones, "Orba is not well, but I promise you that he hears you. Of course, he will obey my father's wishes. Semkah is king of the Meshwesh. Gather the men you need, Thiel, and rest yourself for a few minutes. We will leave within the hour."

"We? You cannot go with us, princess. Not with the Old One in such a state. It is too far a distance, and you are needed here."

I realized he spoke of me, but I had no strength to lie to them. I was waning quickly.

"I *will* go with you. That is not a question—it is my wish. I will not leave my parents stranded in the desert. Is there anything else, Thiel?"

"No, just the stars. They have been falling tonight. We've seen them fall upon the land of Egypt. This does not bode well for our people, I think."

Tears filled my eyes and slid down my wrinkled cheeks. Sumaway dabbed them away before Thiel saw them. "Go now, Thiel," she said quietly. "I will talk to you more soon."

He left us alone, and I grabbed her hand. "When you leave tonight, you will not be coming back. You will go away from here, Sumaway."

She fell down beside me and lay across my chest. "What? How can you know this? This is the sickness talking."

One thing I loved about the princess was that she generally never questioned me. Except for tonight, when she was unsure of everything. She knew I could see in the water, and she believed me. Tonight there was no water, and I had not seen this, but I felt it. Yes, I felt it in my poisoned bones.

"What about my father and mother? Will I find them?"

"I do not know, but I know you must try. Now is the time for the third mekhma. It is your time." Then the fire was upon me, the fire of prophecy. "Ah, yes, you will meet a bull in the desert, Sumaway. You will meet a bull in the desert. Do not leave his side. Where he goes, you go. He will lead you to safety. Go now, and do not look back."

"What about the people, Orba? I cannot leave them to Egypt's hands. What do I do?"

"They must go north, leave the White City. Tell them to go to the sea. But you, you must find the bull."

With a tender kiss on my forehead, she wiped my face once more. "How can I leave you, old friend?"

I tried to laugh, but it came out of my body as a series of coughs. She patted my mouth and tried not to appear shocked at the sight of the dark red blood. I could feel it in my throat and lungs. I was drowning. Drowning in blood. If the potion did not steal my life's breath, the disease would take me soon. For that, I was grateful.

"Easily. I do not want you to see me die. I want to be alone. Go and make your preparations. Send the Council to me. I will tell them my wishes. Go now, Sumaway, last mekhma of the Meshwesh." She squeezed me, and I gasped at the pain but suffered through it for her sake.

She paused in the doorway, and I looked at her one last time. Sumaway was tall, taller than I remembered Nefret or Pah being. She had dark brown hair that sprouted curls around her face. When she was young, she'd enjoyed parading around with no tunic. Now she had a woman's body and was always one to show modesty. She had soft brown eyes like her mother's but a voice like her father's. She had a natural authority and the grace of a seasoned shieldmaiden. She was not as skilled as her sisters with spear and arrow, but she could toss a dagger better than any man. She would be one to be reckoned with if anyone crossed her path. With one last nod and a wave of her hand, she made the sign of respect and vanished from my sight.

I waited for someone else to come. As time passed, I vaguely remembered that the Council was supposed to attend me, but they had not yet appeared. A burst of light filled the room, and from my vantage point, I gathered I'd missed a star shower. Yes, this was a good night to die, with stars heralding my passing. As I struggled to breathe, I thought of Farrah. Why hadn't she come to lead me away? Surely she knew I was close to the Otherworld now. Didn't she care? Had she ever loved me?

I was too tired now to care. I would take one more breath and then let my blood drown me. I wheezed in the darkness and heard the sound of a child's laughter. The room began to brighten as the pain in my chest increased. I struggled to breathe but forgot all about it when I heard the child laughing again. He was somewhere near. I turned my head to look, and there he was. My child! Farrah's child! The son who died so long ago that I could barely remember his name. Had we named him? He had been a fine child too. Strong with a lusty voice. He'd died one night not long after his entrance into this world, and his abrupt leaving had broken my heart. And now he was here to see his father.

What had I called him? What name had I given him when I buried him in the sand? I could not remember, and that brought me great agony. He touched me. He was not a baby anymore but a boy, ready to play with his father. And it did not matter that I could not remember his name, for we were together now. Now he took my hand. How young he was. But this could not be, could it? He had died so long ago, even before Nefret and Pah had been born to Kadeema and Semkah. With his help, I could sit up now. Oh, yes, I could even stand.

And where was Farrah? She should be here to see him. Yes, I always wanted a son.

And now, he was here.

Chapter Five

I found my father in the usual place—in Ipy's lap. The concubine practically set up court in the grape arbor, but I reminded myself again not to become entangled in my parents' ongoing feud over my father's dalliances. Despite my pledge, I found it hard to hide my surprise at seeing the concubine wearing my mother's golden headdress on her head, a prize I was told first belonged to my late aunt Sitamen. Wisely I said nothing about it. I had come with a purpose, and I would not be denied.

I stood before my father's couch and waited for him to stop toying with Ipy's hair like a lovestruck teenager. She wore it in the latest fashion, long dark braids cinched at the ends with gold bands. Gold heaped off her arms and ankles. She looked a royal, or a grotesque caricature of one. My mother never wore such ridiculous amounts of gold. When he finally deigned to notice me, Pharaoh Akhenaten said absently, "Ah, Smenkhkare...where have you been, my son?"

Stymied at his question since he'd been the one to send me away, I evenly answered, "I went to the School of Agility as you instructed, Father. I have come with the token you requested." I held out my wrist and proudly showed him my latest band of achievement. It was proof of my bravery and skill at arms.

"I see you wear another scripted band. This pleases me. Tell me, what does it say?" He sat up now and waited for my answer.

With flushed cheeks, I read the script to him, "Strength is the Soul of Re," I said proudly. "But it is only one of many that I have earned, my father. You have seen the others. This band completes my courses."

"Well done." He rose to his feet, sweeping his blue and white robes to the side as he stretched his back. He waved at me, inviting me to walk with him. My heart cautiously skipped a beat. If I'd pleased him, I could ask him what I wanted. If I was patient and not too overtly clever. He surely couldn't refuse me now.

To my dismay, Ipy walked with us, fanning herself absently with her white plumed fan. She smiled at her ladies, who appeared enthralled by our every move. Some even cast their eyes flirtatiously at me. Despite her attempt at seemingly neutral femininity, Ipy's wearing of my mother's golden headdress made her my foe, whether she understood that or not. I pretended not to notice her attendance in my private conversation with my father. "What do you hope to accomplish next, Smenkhkare? You have done all I ask, and I am pleased with your achievements. How can I reward you?"

"Father, I ask nothing of you. I need nothing, for you have given me everything already."

Ipy nodded her head in approval at my answer, but Father pressed on. "I insist you speak your heart, Smenkhkare. Surely there is something I can give you. Some reward suitable for a prince of Egypt."

"Yes, speak your heart, son of Pharaoh," Ipy said in her simpering voice, "for you know your father to be a good, giving ruler to all his subjects. How much more to his own son? He often speaks of your courage and cleverness with the sword. I am sure he would refuse you nothing."

I found her comments disingenuous, for I did not believe any of their conversations were serious at all. Ipy was notoriously dull-witted, and if it weren't for her pretty face, she would never have caught my father's eye as a young man. Now it seemed their old relationship had been rekindled. I hated that Ipy had inserted herself into our conversation, but as she was my father's concubine, I could only show her honor. "Thank you, Ipy. You are kind to say this, but I know full well what a good and giving man he is. Pharaoh Akhenaten is the best of fathers."

My father walked with his hands behind his back. He was a tall man, taller than I, but in recent months his stomach had taken on a paunch. Still, it seemed the women found him attractive. I knew that my mother loved him a great deal and always smiled in his presence. I wasn't as like him as some of his children were, but I had often been told I had a similar bearing. Taller than most, I spent much of my time stooping down to listen to those around me, but with my father, I tried to stand taller than I was. He smiled as if he read my mind. "You have made a fine son, Smenkhkare. I have always been proud of you." He slapped my back once, and we walked a while without speaking. The ladies trailed us, giggling at whatever it was that amused vapid women. Ipy turned to look at them occasionally to remind them to behave. Finally, he asked, "What of Kames? How is your brother?"

"I am afraid I do not know, Father. I have not spoken to him these many months. He did not join me at the School of Agility." I too was anxious to hear news of Kames, but Father did not offer more information. There had always been tension between them, a tension that had grown as Father had gotten older. I knew he was not my true brother, but we'd been raised together, schooled together and taught to treat one another kindly. At times, Father raised Kames up as a shining example of strength and virility. It was hinted that I should strive to be more like him, but not so much now. I could not fathom Father's ever-changing feelings toward him. Mother was always tight-lipped when it came to Kames, but my grandmother Queen Tiye thought of no one else. If the whole world burned and nobody lived but Kames, it would be enough for her.

There were three brothers in our household. I had another brother, Tutankhamen, but he was Tadukhipa's son and not with us much, except when my Father summoned him to his court. That seemed strange to me since I'd always heard that Tadukhipa had ambition like no other. Surely she would want her fair-faced, pampered son raised near his father? But no, it had not been so. Not until recently. Yes, much had changed recently. Tutankhamen began visiting our sister Meritaten and with a demeanor not acceptable for a brother. I could not allow such a thing to happen. Father could not give my sister to the petulant, spoiled Tutankhamen. That would be the ultimate betrayal. I kept these thoughts buried as my father posed question after question regarding my training. I explained the school's daily regimen of exercise and strength training. He smiled appropriately and nodded at certain points in my description, but I could tell his mind was elsewhere. As mine was.

"I see," he said. We'd left the grape arbor now and took seats in a small pavilion to seek shelter from the afternoon sun. Ipy quickly sat beside him and smiled graciously at me. He waved me to sit at the lower seat. I quietly resented being placed lower than Ipy. If Mother were here, she'd insist that I sit beside Father. "Now that we've walked this way and heard so much about your recent adventures, tell me. What can I give you, son? Your birth celebration approaches, and I want to show all of Egypt how much Pharaoh favors his oldest son."

"Father, there is one thing, if you would consider it. It is such a request that I am loath to ask it, but only you can grant me this." He smiled at me, his dark eyes pleased at my comment. I felt my pulse quicken as I continued. I had to be careful to say the right thing. Diplomacy had never been my strong suit. "You are the sun, and I the son of the sun," I began clumsily. "I think it is time, if you allow it..." I dithered around the subject, but Father patiently waited. Servants approached with wine and a plate of food, but he waved them away as Ipy pouted.

"Please speak your mind, Smenkhkare. I've already said I would not deny you."

With breathless words, I spoke what I'd been longing to say. "I want to marry, Father."

He chuckled knowingly and nodded. "Love strikes us all, doesn't it?" Ipy giggled at his comment. With a grin, he waved the waiting servants forward. They quickly poured and tasted the wine before handing it to him. "I see you are not immune either. For that, I am both delighted and saddened. For in matters of the heart, all men are equal. Even the son of Pharaoh cannot deny love's power."

He drank half a cup of wine before he put it down for the servant to refill it. He appraised me expectantly, looking deep into my eyes as if he'd find the answer to a mystery there. I felt nervous under his scrutiny but didn't flinch. He loved me, of that I was sure. I prayed silently to anyone who would listen: *Please let this happen.* I was suddenly glad that I'd come to Pharaoh first with my request. I knew Mother would not approve of my proposal. No matter how many bands I earned, she wanted me to remain a child at her feet. I was no child but a man.

The older servant handed me a cup and then offered another to Ipy. She batted her eyes at him disapprovingly.

"I envy you, my son. First loves have heat and power unlike any other." He reached for Ipy, who took his hand and kissed it. Was my Father trying to tell me he loved the concubine? Were the rumors true, then? Why would he now do this? Surely there was a reason. I would never have believed my mother to have been capable of being unfaithful, but the news of her affair with Aperel had spread like wildfire throughout the court. I would never say such a thing to Pharaoh, for what if he'd not heard the latest rumor? I could not put my mother in danger. No, I did not believe it. I would not believe it.

I sipped the wine and placed the cup beside me. I did not enjoy wine as some men did. It made me feel reckless and less in control of my tongue. My father drank it day and night, and I'd never heard him misspeak once. "So, who is it that has stolen my son's heart so completely? A daughter of Salilah, perhaps? I hear her daughters are exquisite, and all skilled musicians. Perhaps one of Ipy's daughters?"

"No, Father. Although your daughters are fair, lady. And I do not know these daughters of Salilah, although I have heard of their beauty. It is Meritaten I speak of, Pharaoh. I love her and want to marry her."

In a sudden rush, Pharaoh rumbled to his feet, slamming his half-empty cup on the marble-topped table. Ipy froze, ignoring the wine that splashed across her chest.

"You dare ask me this? Was this the queen's idea?"

"No! It is my own heart that asks, Father. I love Meritaten. I have not told my mother about my intentions. How have I offended you?" I did not know how to move or what to say. Fear fell on me as I winced under Pharaoh's anger.

"You think to take your sister, my daughter, to wife? Do you intend to also ask for my kingdom? For that is what it sounds like!"

At the implication, Ipy also stood, and her hand flew to her mouth. "No!" she shouted in surprise. She rushed to Pharaoh's side and steadied him with her hand.

"Never! Never would I dream such a thing, my father and Pharaoh! Please, have mercy! I withdraw my request."

He walked away from me, his fists clenched. Ipy dogged his heels and glanced back at me nervously. She waved at me to stay where I was. I could not hear her words, but she touched his arm and leaned into his ear. He ducked away from her at first, but she persisted until eventually he returned to me. His handsome face was lined with anger, his dark eyes two hard rivets showing no recognition that I was his own flesh and blood. With one word, he could kill me. And he might. Many who loved Pharaoh also died by his hand.

He stood with his hands on his hips, staring me down. I thought for one second he would strike me down with the back of his hand. I'd heard of my father's hot temper, but until recently, it had never been directed at me. Not like this. To think it would turn on me so was more than I could bear. I cast my eyes down ashamedly. I lost all hope that I would have Meritaten. She would never be mine. I'd failed her.

"Lady Ipy has spoken on your behalf, Smenkhkare. She is right, of course. You are a man now and have a man's needs. It is not right that Pharaoh's son should satisfy himself with the flesh of whores and commoners. You deserve a royal wife."

I could hardly believe my ears. Was he saying he would grant me my wish? I lifted my head slowly but did not rise to my feet. I would remain on my knees until told otherwise.

"Thank you, Father! It is all I ever wanted," I whispered nervously, staring at his sandals.

He stared at me again and said evenly, "I will not give you Meritaten. I have already made plans for her. I will, however, give you someone with patience who can teach you how to be a husband. Someone with a lovely face and a pleasing voice."

Again Ipy appeared, this time whispering in Father's ear. He nodded with a smile. "You may have your sister, Ipy's daughter, Ankhesenamun. She is not promised to anyone and will make an excellent wife."

I stood swaying under the weight of his words. How could he do this? This was not fair! I could not help but speak my heart. "As you say, Father, love has no master. I love Ankhesenamun as my sister, but not as a wife. How can I marry her?"

My father stepped toward me. He was so close now I could reach out and touch him. "You will not have my kingdom yet, Smenkhkare. You will take Ankhesenamun as your wife. That is the end of it. That is my word. Go now."

I rose awkwardly and stepped back, bringing my fist to my heart in a show of obedience and spun around, leaving him behind.

As I stepped away, the fear of Pharaoh abated, and I began to feel desperation rise. And then anger. So desperate was I that I began to weigh my options. How could I refuse Ankhesenamun and risk my father's wrath? How would I live without Meritaten?

With every step, I felt my resolution growing. Yes, I would go to my mother, the Great Queen! She would have to help me. I was her son! I could never marry a daughter of Ipy!

I would take my case to her and pray she still had enough influence to change his mind. I would not tell Meritaten of my failure, not yet, but I could not wait long. Court gossip, especially news of an impending marriage, would travel quickly.

If I could not have Meritaten, I would not marry. I would risk my father's wrath, but I would die if I had to. My cause was just.

Yes, I would go to Mother and plead for her help. I would do anything she asked, even rid her of Ipy.

I had to do this rather than break my own Meritaten's heart. And hers was the only heart that mattered.

Chapter Six

Queen of Despair—Nefertiti

Queen Tiye dawdled into my chamber this morning before my bath, her face askew with worry. "Where have you hidden the baby, Desert Queen? Where is Kames? Give me Kames."

I pulled the robe back on and came to her. I held her bony hand in mine and patted it. "He is a baby no longer, Great Queen. He is a man now and in Pharaoh's service. He has gone on a diplomatic trip to the west. You will see him soon."

I led her to a nearby padded couch. I couldn't believe she'd arrived unattended and in the shape she was in. She wore no wig, and her natural hair, thin and curly, sprang up around her face like an unruly cloud. She'd slept in her makeup—slick streaks of kohl slid down the side of her face, and her lips were ringed with stiff red paint.

"Oh, yes, I remember now. What of Thutmose? Has he come home yet?" She spoke now of her own son, dead at least twenty-five years.

I could not break her heart again this morning, so I told her a pleasant lie instead. I knew the pain of losing a child. I had lost three myself, and the grief never left me. "No, Great Queen. He is still away, but he too will return soon. For now, it is just you and me." I squeezed her hand and poured her a cup of water, which she accepted.

Her hands shook, but she drank the water until the cup was empty. Setting it on the table, she took in the view of the room. "I like this room. I've always liked this room. It feels very cool in here, and there are no bats. I dislike bats."

"Yes, it is very cool here. And I never see bats. Are you hungry, Queen Tiye?"

"No, I am not." She rubbed at her nose with her finger and eyed me. "My son is very lucky to have you, Nefertiti."

What to say to that? If she were whole and hale, I'd beg her for help. I'd throw myself at her feet and plead with her to speak to her son for me. But she was not. This was only a fragile shell of the intelligent, quick-witted, sometimes cruel woman I knew. And as far as I knew, Akhenaten no longer allowed her in his court. We were like two cast-off queens, forgotten and wished dead. Such a sad ending, but it wasn't really the end, was it? Pah's words from last night rang in my mind, and I had tried all morning to pretend none of it had happened. How could I leave the people I loved behind? Tiye needed me. It was she who had brought me here. She'd been the very Hand of Destiny that led the Falcon of the Red Lands to the throne of Egypt. Now she was losing her mind and had no one to care for her. When Huya was living he took great pains to hide her condition, but now that the old man was gone, there was no one else. No one she would trust. Except me.

"I hear the Hittite witch returns with her son today. I wonder what misery she will bring with her?"

I smiled at her. Not because of her insult toward Tadukhipa but because it was evidence that at least some part of her mind worked well enough to recall her hatred for Kiya, the Monkey, as she liked to call our sister-queen to her face.

"Oh? I had not heard that," I lied prettily and bit a piece of fruit.

"Then you are in trouble. You should know every soul who passes through the gate and when they leave again. It is not enough to hide here in your comfortable room, Nefertiti. You must rule your kingdom. Knowledge is everything. When I was your age, I knew daily who came into the kitchens, who slept with my servants—and my husband. And who approached my husband's throne for favors. You must have eyes everywhere if you hope to see the enemy come toward you. If you fail to do so, you will no longer be Great Queen but only the Queen of Despair."

"I know this, Mother. I am just tired this morning." Unexpectedly she pinched me under my arm and stood to her feet. "Ow!" I gasped at the pain.

"Good! I am glad that hurt you. That will be nothing compared to what Tadukhipa will do. She'll no doubt insist that her puny son be married to one of your daughters. I have heard this." Her superior knowledge must have stirred her hunger because she reached for a piece of fruit too. "What will you do?"

Desperately I whined, "What can I do? Your son has taken Ipy to his bed and refuses to speak to me for more than a few seconds. I think he's never forgiven me for Kames." Queen Tiye snorted at that comment. It was refreshing to talk to her like this. I wasn't sure how long it would last, so I took advantage of her keen mind while it was still available to me. "I should have kept silent that day, the day when he announced that I was Great Queen. It was enough that you'd claimed the boy. I thought that with time, Akhenaten would change his mind about Kames. Instead, he's come to resent me, but I can't think why. He loved his sister, and I think he also loved Ramose."

"Not enough to save them," she said, tossing the apple core onto the silver platter.

"No, not enough to save them," I agreed, glancing at Menmet as she entered to tidy up my room. Queen Tiye growled at her like a dog, something she'd never done before, and I waved Menmet away.

"I do not like that girl. She has the look of her father, Heby. She has his spirit too. You are wrong to trust her."

"Great Queen, she has been my friend for fifteen years and never once has betrayed me. And she hates her father. Why would you growl at her?" I said with a laugh.

She did not answer my question but just snorted. "Then you are stupid, and I cannot help you."

I did not argue with her further. I pretended not to worry about the time. Adijah would visit me today in the Queen's Court. Unfortunately, he might be waiting a while. I couldn't hurry the queen.

I hunkered down in the chair, unsure what to do now. *Oh, Akhenaten, how could you abandon us so? We are the women who love you!*

"I saw the stars fall last night, Nefertiti. I know that evil has fallen upon us and that it comes on the bottom of Tadukhipa's sandals. If you have any sense about you, you will refuse her entrance into the palace this morning. Keep her away, for she will be the death of me, Nefertiti! And you too! She hates us all. She hates Akhenaten too!" Her eyes widened with strong emotion, and she began wringing her hands and rocking back and forth.

"Calm yourself, Great Queen. All will be well."

"How can you say that? Nothing will be well again. And where is Kames, Nefertiti? I do not hear the baby. Give him to me."

I bit my lip. Queen Tiye was becoming agitated now. "Why don't you go prepare to greet him, Great Queen? Ask your servants to prepare your finest clothes and dress your hair. I will send him to you when he returns, but we must be ready."

"Yes." She smiled weakly and stood. She gathered the ends of her dingy gown in her hand and walked toward the arched entrance doors of my chambers. "And you will send him to me?"

"Of course," I said, smiling at her comfortingly.

"Very well, but do not forget what I told you." I could see by her expression that she herself had already forgotten her own words.

"Yes, Great Queen." I rose as she left me and watched her disappear into the corridor. "Menmet! Help me dress. I will have to skip the bath this morning. My guests will be waiting for me."

"I don't see why you can't make them wait. They are just Grecians, and you are the Great Queen," she said testily. She was obviously still angry that Tiye had growled at her, but she'd have to keep her opinions to herself. More than once lately, I'd had to remind Menmet that she was not to speak her mind so freely. What if someone heard her disparage Tiye or another member of the royal family? It would cost her her life, and I was in no position to help her.

"Hush now. I'll do the brushing. Find me something blue to wear."

"Yes, lady." She scurried off while I tugged at my nest of tangles. Tonight, I would do as Pah asked—I would cut my hair. I would shave it away. Could I really do that? It was the one thing that Akhenaten still loved about me. *Are you going to let your vanity keep you in danger, Nefret?* I heard my sister's question ringing in my ears. No, I would not. I would do whatever it took to protect my children.

"Lady, your son is outside and wants to see you."

I put the brush down and couldn't hide my surprise. "Smenkhkare has returned? Since when? Yes, of course. Let him in." I stood and tidied my gown. I gathered my loose hair and wrapped it around my hand before I tossed it over one shoulder. Smenkhkare hurried into the room, so anxious was he to see me. He was the spitting image of his father as a younger man, and in a strange way, he reminded me of someone else too. *Alexio!* My mind whispered the answer. It made sense. He had some of the Red Lands blood in his veins too. Why wouldn't he have the look of our people?

With a polite bow of his head, he smiled at me, and for a moment, all was right with the world. Until I looked into his eyes. He was hurting deeply. "Have you eaten, son? You look well. I see you wear a new band. Let me see it." I showered him with smiles and invited him to sit with me.

"Is there anyone else here, Mother? I need to speak with you most urgently."

"No one is here, except Menmet. What is it?" My skin crawled for a moment. I hoped he was not here to confront me about the rumors. I knew what they were saying about Aperel and me, but it simply wasn't true. And Tiye was right—I saw Tadukhipa's hand in that evil gossip.

"I need your help, Mother."

I leaned forward and grasped his hands. They felt rough and strong, a warrior's hands. When he didn't soften under my touch, I released them. He wasn't a child anymore, and I couldn't treat him like one. "What is it, son? What has happened? Is it your father?"

"Yes and no." Smenkhkare's face tensed as he spoke. The grooves around his mouth deepened, and his young brow furrowed slightly. "Must you always think of him? He's not worthy of you, Mother."

"Hush now, Smenkhkare. Do not speak so meanly of your father. He is Pharaoh. And," I whispered, "we are never alone."

He nodded. "I am sorry, but the worst thing has happened. I finished the School of Agility. I did all that he asked of me. He offered me a prize, but he will not give me what I want. Instead, he has done the unthinkable! I cannot do what he asks!"

"My son! Why are you so upset? It cannot be as bad as all that. Can it?"

"He was with Ipy, of course. He is like her lap dog, I think." He paced the room now, uncaring that my servant was nearby. "He offered me a prize, said he wanted to honor me before all Egypt. The only prize I wanted was, well, I asked him for Meritaten's hand, and he refused me. I am to marry Ipy's daughter instead. He accused me of trying to steal his kingdom! Can you imagine that? I am his son! Why would I steal what is rightfully mine? Please, Mother. I do not know what has passed between you and my father, but can't you help me now? Surely you see that Meritaten and I should be together."

In my tribe, brothers did not marry their sisters, but I had long ago abandoned my revulsion for these unions. This was the Egyptian way, at least for royals, and my disapproval would not change that. And if Meritaten did not marry a brother or her father, there would be no one else for her. She might even end up like Sitamen. I shivered at the thought.

"She loves me and I her. We know that we are meant to be together. Now that will not happen. Please, go to Father and plead my case. He will listen to you."

"No, he will not, son. You should have come to me first, Smenkhkare. Now that Pharaoh has spoken, there is nothing to be done. You will have Ipy's daughter as a wife, but do not lose hope. Pharaoh's sons have many wives. It may be that you will have Meritaten in time. Prove to him that he can trust you. No doubt others have whispered suspicions in his ears."

"What could they possibly whisper? I have done *everything*!" He slammed his fist down on the table and glared at me. "And this is your answer? Can't you see what misery your passiveness has brought us already? His concubine struts about wearing one of your crowns, and you do nothing. She's bending his ear to her demands, and he's obeying her as if she were the master and he the slave!"

"Careful!" I said vehemently. "Do not take that tone with me. You don't know what I have said or done. Do you think I command Akhenaten? Have I ever been able to do so? You are foolish to believe it."

"Yet he does as *she* commands. It was she who commanded me to take Ankhesenamun. Don't you care?"

I felt great sadness to hear such a report, and even greater sadness to see my son's disappointment, but there was no solution. "As I said, there is nothing I can do now. You must be patient."

"I guess the rumors are true, then. You have fallen out of favor—and why? Because you couldn't keep your hands off Aperel?"

I shot to my feet at hearing such words coming out of my son's mouth. How could he believe such lies about me?

"Will you bring us all to ruin now, Mother?"

I slapped my son across the face. How dare he repeat evil palace gossip in my hearing! Wounded, he towered over me as if he were tempted to strike me back. Tears burned my eyes, but I would not release them over such lies. And to hear them from my own son's mouth! Without another word, Smenkhkare stormed out of my room. I heard a clattering of trays in the outer chamber, evidence of his anger.

"Lady? Are you all right? Has he harmed you?"

"Leave me, Menmet. Tell my guests I will not see them now. I have to...I have matters of state to attend to. See that they are entertained and assure them that I will see them this evening."

With a bow, she said, "Yes, lady. I will go now."

As she left me alone, I slid out of my clothing and into the bath. There was a razor nearby. It shone brilliantly in the bright sunshine that filtered through the many windows. All it would take would be one swipe—no, two swipes—and the life would seep out of me. As quickly as I entertained the idea, I dismissed it. I would never do such a thing. I wanted to see my children again, my mother, others who had passed. If I took a life, even my own, that would weigh against me. No, this was not an option.

I sank into the water and let it cover my head. The tears wouldn't come, but my heart was broken. As I emerged from the water, my hair sticking to my body, I heard a sweet sound. I had not heard it in many years: short, chirpy trills, and a long one. It was the song of the Bee-Eater! Then I spotted him. He bounced on my windowsill, witnessing my nakedness with no fear or timidity.

This was the sign I'd been promised! There was no denying it! After a few moments, he burst into song again and suddenly flew away. I eased out of the bath and dried my body, patting it with a fresh linen towel.

Yes, it was time. I retrieved the razor and began hacking at my hair. I did not have much time. Menmet would be gone for a while, making the arrangements for Adijah and his company. I did as Pah instructed. As I sliced, I dumped the hair into a basket, one that I would burn on my own. No one must know what I was doing. No one could know.

Finally, as I clumsily shaved my head, I wept. My image in the polished bronze mirror was more than I could bear. I wept harder.

Now I was truly the Queen of Despair.

Chapter Seven

A New God—Akhenaten

"Horemheb has left the palace at the queen's command, and he was not alone."

I leaned toward Saho and kept one eye on my wife as she approached my throne. It was a formal entrance, but this had been my wish for today. It was a special day, as she would soon discover.

"And?"

"Kames accompanied him. They left this morning."

I waved Saho back and watched Nefertiti now. My skin burned with the heat of my anger. I felt Ipy's eyes upon me, but I was riveted on my wife's cool exterior. She might make these others believe all was well, but I knew her. I knew inside she was twisting, like a battle banner caught in a strong wind. And I was the storm bringer! How could I have been so foolish to trust her? Against all my father taught me, I allowed my heart to lead my mind. My counselors had been correct from the beginning—she would betray me. She was not an Egyptian and not of royal blood. I believed now that she couldn't help but lie, she was of the corrupt Red Lands blood. They were all crooks and worse. And there was no truth in her. It was lucky for her that I did not drag Aperel's dead body through the court since I heard she loved him so well.

To make matters stickier and far more threatening, her sister—whom she called Pah but whom all Egypt knew as Nephthys, the high priestess of the Green Temple of Isis—now assisted her in her schemes. Nephthys had lied to me before the court, and whether she knew it or not, she'd placed herself in grave danger.

If I believed the priestess, the recent celestial display meant nothing more significant than that my kingdom would soon be awash with the glory of the heavens. That heaven would soon come to earth and my "Golden Kingdom," as she called it, would be established forever.

Anyone with sense knew that the falling stars signified something important—something evil—but she had acted as if nothing was amiss. She'd cast those solemn green eyes upon me, and I wanted to believe her, so like my wife was she, only she appeared untouched by time. As far as I knew, she'd never been a mother, and her thin waist attested to this observation. The differences between the sisters were slight. Only someone with a gift for observation would be able to identify them correctly, but I'd been studying people all my life. Discerning their true identities was a talent I prided myself in.

With hooded eyes, I studied Nefertiti as she bowed before me. As everyone in attendance expected, I waved my hand and invited her to sit beside me. With some hesitation, she walked up the dais and took her seat on her gold and turquoise throne. Once she settled into place, the rest of the court gathered around us to witness the formal announcement. I'd not been kind to Nefertiti, and I'd not allowed anyone to prepare her for what was to come. I longed to hurt her as she'd hurt me. I wanted to see her writhe in her place before my royal court.

And now it began. As planned, Ipy came before us first and fell to her knees with her ceremonial bowl upraised above her head. This traditional birth announcement might not shock my wife, but it was only the first in a series of blows I was set to deliver. "Bless me, Daughter of Isis. I am with child," she purred to my wife in her childlike voice. To my utter disappointment, Nefertiti did not blink or hesitate in acknowledging Ipy. She accepted the pitcher of water from Saho's hand and walked down the stairs.

I could not see her face, as she had her back to me, but she did everything that was expected of her. She poured the water into the bowl and said in a pleasant voice, "I, Nefertiti, the Daughter of Isis, also called Neferneferuaten by my loving sovereign and husband Akhenaten, bless you, Ipy. May your child be born with beauty, health, and wisdom as befitting the child of our sovereign, Akhenaten. Rise and be blessed." Nefertiti passed the pitcher to her servant Menmet and graciously helped Ipy to her feet. Ipy drank from the bowl, accepting the blessing of the Great Queen. Then, to everyone's surprise, Nefertiti hugged the concubine as if she were greeting a long-lost relative. Applause thundered through the court at the unexpected show of affection.

Once decorum was restored, Nefertiti spoke in a commanding voice that was a beautiful mask. "Come now, Ipy. Take a seat of honor beside our Pharaoh. The goddess has blessed your womb with precious life. In you is the seed of our Pharaoh's greatness."

The gathering clapped respectfully now as Ipy and Nefertiti ascended the steps together. I glared at them both, and Nefertiti calmly glided toward me and stood beside my throne as if to remind me of her place here. I could feel the tide of sentiment turning in Nefertiti's favor. Ipy's smile seemed silly compared to Nefertiti's serene expression. Ipy had no idea what had just happened. She glanced at me expectantly as she rubbed her stomach and smiled stupidly. I felt Nefertiti's hand on my shoulder, and it felt like flame on my skin. How could I still love her? How was it possible to feel the depth of hatred that I felt, yet yearn for her so intensely that I would even now forgive her if she would only ask me? Aggravated by my sentimentality, I waved to Saho to continue the order of events.

Somehow Nefertiti had known what I planned, and she knew what to do. Someone had betrayed me, and my wife, the Great Queen, outplayed me. Once again, I could not give Ipy what she wanted most, to be named the wife of Pharaoh. Her expectant expression did nothing to persuade me. Instead, I waved my hand again, signaling for the service to move along quickly. Suddenly, the shiny gold doors of the court opened once more, glinting like flames in the midday sun.

"But..." Ipy whispered to her handmaiden. One look from me and she said nothing else. This at least I would do. I would not allow my wife to steal this moment from me. She would not have my son. If he wanted to marry, let him also learn how to rule. Today I would make my son co-regent. It would be a symbolic gesture but one that would surely capture his loyalty like a bird in a snare. Never again would he plot against me with his mother, as I knew he had earlier. He did not approve of my judgment, but he would soon learn who was the master here.

"Come forward, Smenkhkare. The throne recognizes you." I felt Nefertiti shift nervously beside me. *Ah, so she did not know this.*

That knowledge pleased me greatly. Smenkhkare's tall frame reminded me of someone I had not thought of in a long time. How much he looked like Thutmose! It was truly uncanny. The sight of him made me shiver, but I leaned forward and summoned the young man closer. He closed the distance quickly and knelt in humility. He also had no clue why he'd been summoned to the Court of the Aten. Birds chirped and a cloud flitted across the open pavilion, casting a small shadow over the affair. It did not stay long, and the murmuring it caused ceased with just one look from my prophet, Saho.

"Today, my son Smenkhkare, firstborn of my sons and son of the Great Queen Nefertiti, I bestow upon you the honor of co-regent. Rise now and be crowned."

The crowd gasped at the astonishing news. The effect gave me great pleasure.

Smenkhkare raised his eyes to me, wide and filled with surprise. I smiled at him, and the servant came quickly to my side. The boy journeyed up the steps and knelt again, this time at my feet. He whispered, "You honor me beyond my worthiness, Father."

"You are my son and indeed worthy. Rise now, Smenkhkare, co-regent of Upper and Lower Egypt. Let Egypt look upon you and all your splendor." The boy breathed hard once and rose with his chin held high. With a determined look, he faced the crowd and accepted their applause and cheers. Ipy removed herself from the throne beside me, with the help of Saho, and I led Smenkhkare to the vacant seat.

"Forever as one we are, father and son, obedient to the Aten for eternity."

As he took his throne, he said in response, "For eternity, my father and Pharaoh. Obedient to the Aten."

The crowd roared, tears on their faces, and even Nefertiti applauded joyfully. Did she not understand that she would never again sit upon the Great Throne of Egypt? I gripped the carved handgrips on my throne and glared at her. The mother of my children, the stealer of my heart. The cheers of my court did not gladden my soul. I rose and raised my hands in the sign of the Aten. I blessed the people as was my custom during these formal affairs. Let them cheer for my son. I was tired of them. All of them. All I wanted to do was disappear, perhaps lose myself in worship to the Aten. Yes, I would become one with the Aten. I needed none of these mortals. I would be one with my god.

Despite my desire to avoid her face, I was to be denied. "Please, Akhenaten. Wait. We must talk." Nefertiti shuffled behind me. She wore all gold today. The color had always suited her, unlike Ipy.

"What now?" I waved my attendants away and faced the woman I had once loved with all my soul, all my being.

"Thank you for what you have done. Appointing Smenkhkare as co-regent is a wise move. He is worthy of your trust."

I smirked at her. "So, you acknowledge that I outplayed you? You thought you would steal my son's love?"

"What? Never would I do such a thing. I want only the best for our children, all of them. And...I love you, Akhenaten. I have not stopped loving you, even though it has been many moons since you have come to see me. Or come to my bed. It's not too late, my husband. We can fix whatever is broken between us. We are young still."

"Not so young, I think. I hear you can no longer bear children."

She drew back, the hurt in her eyes plain. "Who would say such a thing? It is not true." Her eyes shimmered with tears, but they did not melt my heart. I'd seen tears before. "And why would you believe such lies? Why have you not come to me to ask me yourself? I know you blame me for the death of our daughter, but I too feel the loss. She was my child too, husband."

Ignoring the pain in her voice, I said, "A wife who can no longer bear children is of no use to a Pharaoh—or a god."

Her carefully painted green eyes widened at my words. "What are you saying? Do you plan to declare yourself a god now? Why would you do such a thing? That goes against everything we've believed in, everything we've worked for! Would you abandon all that you've done? You remember what you said, Akhenaten. Freedom to choose, freedom to worship. Those were your words. By doing this, you'd be no better than the priests of Amun." She touched my arm, and her hand felt cool. Her words stung, but I let her touch me. I missed her touch. Over the past months, my heart had traveled too far away from her, too far to go back now. "Please, speak to me, my love. I feel as if someone has poisoned your mind against me. We are one, are we not?"

I could smell her scent, a blend of sweet cinnamon, white lotus, and something else that was indefinable. Only she wore this scent, and it drove me mad.

"We were once."

Her jaw quivered as she whispered, "Where did we go wrong, Akhenaten? What happened? I must know."

I stepped closer to her, closed my eyes, and breathed her in one last time. Yes, one last time. Then I would banish her from my sight and my heart forever. "The bastard child, Aperel and, of course, your Red Lands lover, Alexio. How often you spoke his name while you slept in my bed."

"What?" She gasped in surprise.

I touched her face with my hand and stroked her jaw for a moment before I clenched her throat. She did not fight me. "You thought I didn't know, but I knew. I always knew. I forgave you because you were young and foolish, but then you took Aperel to your bed. I saw you two talking, your heads bent together, conspiring against me. You cannot deny it, Desert Queen."

"I do deny it!" she said in a hoarse whisper. Smacking my hand furiously, she took her life in her hands. My guards stepped closer, but I waved them away. "Aperel never betrayed you, and you murdered him. It's as if I do not know you at all! Since I've been your wife, I have been true to you, husband. Yes! I was true while you took more wives and concubines. You have openly shamed me with your dalliances and liaisons, yet I've said nothing! I hoped you would come to your senses and remember who we are, what we hoped to do."

"How dare you speak to me about shame? You shame me by bringing the deceiver's child into my court, practically nursing him at your breast. Have *you* no shame?"

"Kames? Can't you even say his name?"

"You knew I didn't want him here, yet you claimed him, you made him our son. The bastard son of my disobedient general and his Meshwesh whore! It is because of him that Sitamen is dead! And you made him our son. What do you care about shaming our house?"

"He was a child! I didn't kill Sitamen, the priests did. And you let them!"

Fury rose in me like the River Nile, and I slapped her across her face. It immediately left a vicious palm print on her pale skin. Although she clapped a hand over it, she did not back down.

"Go ahead! You can kill me too! That would solve everything, wouldn't it? You could raise up a new queen, one who would simper and roll over like a dog whenever you spoke. I promise you this, husband. She does not have your best in mind."

"What do you know? If it's Ipy you speak of, you must know I have always loved her. I loved her long before I laid eyes on you," I lied through gritted teeth. "Long before my mother paraded you before me like a foreign prize. It is time to do what is right for Egypt, Nefertiti."

Swinging her robes behind her, she said, "From this day forward, I am no longer Nefertiti. I am Nefret. Kill me now, if you like, or kill me later. It is no matter to me. I see now that my husband, the great Akhenaten, is dead."

I flinched at her declaration. It was a grievous sin to speak of death so loosely, especially in reference to a pharaoh. It was as if she had declared a death sentence on me. The others around us hissed their disapproval, but she did not seem to notice.

She spun on her heel and left me gaping after her. As she walked away, I had the curious sensation that I'd witnessed this before. In a dream, perhaps. I couldn't explain it, but I knew one thing.

I would never see her again.

Chapter Eight

A Golden Son—Tadukhipa

A portly steward led me into my chambers as if I'd forgotten where they were, and I frowned, thinking of what I would tell the Hittite king about this newest turn of events. My father was dead, and my uncle now ruled, but that would not help me. Long ago I had been given a task, and I had failed. After all these years Akhenaten was no closer to elevating me than he had been at the beginning of our marriage.

They should have listened to me and killed the red-haired witch while they had the chance. I dismissed the steward and sat at the table while I watched my scribe set up his pens and papyrus. Of course, one of my husband's court was attending this meeting, so I could not express my true heart in any of these matters. He would report whatever I wrote, as was the tradition, but venting my frustration would not help me. No one helped Tadukhipa. I always helped myself.

But at long last, I would have some measure of revenge on this court. That I had decided. I could not leave this world or face an ousting by Ipy without exacting my revenge on the Old Queen. Even now my faithful servant was procuring my method of torture for use against my old rival. This would certainly close the lid on her sarcophagus. To my surprise, my husband Akhenaten came to see me. His scribe and I rose and bowed before him, and I waited until he spoke my name. It had been the longest of times since I'd had a visit from him. I was both delighted and terrified, for according to the recent reports, his moods were very changeable as of late.

"Wife, forgive my intrusion," he said in his smooth, deep voice.

"Never say it. You are always welcome here, lord and pharaoh. Please allow me to pour wine for you." He nodded and took my vacant seat. "Go, scribe. You are not needed now," I said in a pleasant yet stern voice. With my own hands, I poured the cup, sipped it, and passed it to him. He also sipped the wine but then extended his arms to me.

Indeed, this is unusual.

He held me close to him and kissed my cheek before releasing me. "I was pleased to see you in court today."

"Your invitation to attend honors me. I would never refuse an invitation from you, my lord." I smiled sweetly and took a position next to him at the table. *And yet you hardly summon me and didn't blink when I asked to retire to the Royal Harem, away from you and your Desert Queen.*

"You could have refused, but you chose to honor my son Smenkhkare. It was a deed that did not go unnoticed. Is that hawk necklace worn in his honor?" As he smiled, the grooves around his mouth deepened. Yes, he was handsome still. Did I feel affection for him? Was it true? Did I actually love Akhenaten? No, that couldn't be possible. I would never allow my heart to behave so foolishly. I suddenly felt old and unattractive. Perhaps I was.

"Of course. What a handsome, intelligent young man! He will surely make an excellent regent. And I am sure his mother was pleased as well." I couldn't resist the dig, but Akhenaten did not take the bait. However, I saw a shadow pass over his handsome face. *So, the rumors are true! The Desert Queen has lost her power over him. Perhaps now he will do as he has always promised. He will make me Great Queen!*

"Although it is always pleasant to visit with you, I have a purpose for my visit today."

"Yes?" I said with great anticipation.

"I have not forgotten my second son, Tutankhamen. I have been thinking of the future, Tadukhipa. He too is to be honored before Egypt. I have decided to make him the Hawk Prince, now that his brother is co-regent. He will serve as honorary regent during special events and when his older brother Smenkhkare is away from court. This is my desire."

"Then it shall be so." I smiled politely, my heart sinking. *So, nothing for me, then?*

"I thought you would be pleased. He is a fine boy. A credit to my house. And he has your wit, although I say at times it is very sharp for one so young. I will announce this soon, but I wanted to tell you first so you could prepare the boy for his duties."

"He will no doubt be as deeply honored as I am by whatever honors you bestow upon him. Thank you for your kindness to our son, Akhenaten." With a gulp, he finished his drink and walked out of the room, pausing at the doorway as I called to him. "Please, husband. Come see me soon. My arms are hungry for you," I said, feeling a rare measure of vulnerability. To my own surprise I meant those words. Without looking at me, he nodded once and left me alone.

I twisted the edge of my gown and ran to my bed, collapsing in a heap. I screamed into my pillow, the frustration and anger welling up inside me. I beat the pillows with my fists but refused to cry. I gasped for air and finally rolled on my back. *He honors my son but not me. Never me. I have nothing for all the emptiness. For all the loneliness. I have nothing. Even now when Nefertiti's star falls, I have nothing.*

How tired I was of hearing her name and seeing their weird statues. It was as if the artists were portraying them as one being. Others could not see it, but I did. But apparently, that wasn't so anymore. Her image was no longer the object of every artist's rendering. For that, at least, I was thankful. I dreamed of taking a chisel to her face, a hammer to the stonework, pounding it into dust. I hadn't been alone in my shock and surprise. The entire court gasped when the new paintings appeared a few years ago. The portrayal of Akhenaten's strong, masculine figure as an effeminate, misshapen monster had offended everyone. Surely this had been her idea, they whispered, and I agreed. The Desert Queen wanted nothing more than to destroy Akhenaten. What better way than to present him as a monster to his people?

I slid into my sandals, tidied my wig, and went into the hall A phalanx of servants fell in behind me. I'd chosen to wear pink this morning. Pink had been Tiye's favorite color before she lost her mind.

I hated the color, but I wore it to offend her, as I knew it would. In a few hours, when the night fell on Pharaoh's city, Mure would fill the Old Queen's chamber with bats. Oh, how she hated those creatures! I smiled at the idea. I had long planned to present her with such a surprise, but I had to wait until Akhenaten no longer cared so much for his mother. And indeed, now he did not. I couldn't remember the last time he had visited her. That pleased me greatly.

I prayed I would hear her screams all the way in my chamber. That would be an excellent turn of events.

I strolled past the Great Queen's chambers, not bothering to offer my greetings, and continued into the smaller, less impressive rooms. I hoped to find Ipy and to find her alone. I was not disappointed. She stood immediately when she saw me, bowed angrily, and then crossed her arms like a spoiled child who'd missed her evening treat. Ipy had plump arms and full breasts. It had been a long time since she'd been pregnant. Her daughters were old enough to marry now, and yet here she was again, having another one of Pharaoh's children. It seemed so unfair.

I'd had three children. Tutankhamen and Ankhesenamun lived, but my third child had died in my womb. I thought I would die then, so great had been the pain in my heart and my body. But I had lived. Lived long enough to see Ipy raised from the harem into the queen's courts. Even though she was not yet a queen of Akhenaten, it was only a matter of time. Now I'd obviously caught her in the midst of a tantrum. She'd been throwing things about, having a fit. Without interruption, she continued.

"He promised! He promised me!" The clanging of brass cups and breaking dishes filled the open space. Confused servants lingered back, unwilling to stop their mistress from destroying Pharaoh's treasures.

"Here now! Is there a war I have not been told about?" I asked her loudly, with some amusement.

"What are you doing here? Have you come to gloat?"

"Why should I gloat over your disappointment, Ipy? It is nothing to me."

She pulled her hair from her face and straightened her back. She stalked toward me, her fists clenched. I did not act afraid. What would I fear? She might strike me. I hoped she did so that I could have her killed. To strike a queen of Egypt would mean her death. She remembered in time to save herself. "I ask again," she said, baring her teeth at me, "why have you come?"

"I came to offer you my friendship, Ipy. It seems you are in need of friends these days."

"What do you know about me, Queen Kiya?"

My back prickled at hearing the old insult. "Call me what you will, but I have a crown on my head. What do you have, Ipy? Should I tell you the names they call you behind your back?"

"What names?"

Oh, how easy this is! She took the bait without being pushed!

"Let's see. I think I've heard 'Ipy the Squint-Eyed' most recently. It is true that you struggle to see, isn't it? You do squint quite a bit. It is most unattractive."

She kicked a tall brass brazier. Luckily for her, there were no coals inside, or else she would have caught herself on fire.

"Shall I tell you what they call you, then? Sister?"

"You are no sister of mine, Ipy. You are not queen yet. But perhaps we can solve that problem. Perhaps I can speak to my husband for you."

That quieted her. "I don't believe you would do that. Why would you?"

"I don't know why you don't believe it. I do such things for my friends."

"I have heard about your friends, Tadukhipa. I have no need or desire for such friends." Her intimation was clear. She referred to my Inhapi and the few who followed her. Fine! Let her mock me. Let her see what love in this court was all about.

"Having me as an enemy would be a mistake, Ipy." I rubbed the head of a gold lion as I glanced up at her. "A very big mistake. Why don't we work together? You can have what you want, and I can have what I want. It makes sense. That is how things work here. Those who advance must work with others. You must work with me, or else you will be left behind."

She snorted at me. "You mean, *you'll* be left behind. I have no doubt that Akhenaten will make me queen, perhaps even Great Queen. I do not need your help, Tadukhipa. You see I have done well for myself, and you have never helped me before. Why start now?" She did not wait for an answer but continued, her voice dropped in a mocking tone, "I know why. Because it is you who cannot accomplish your task. How long have you been a lowly queen? You let the outsider take your place, and now I will take hers and yours. Make no mistake, Queen Tadukhipa. I am not your friend. I will never be your friend. Now get out."

My servants gasped behind me. What a low, common woman to speak to me in such a way. I felt at my hip, but my blade was not there. Instead, I grabbed her arms and pulled her to me. We were nose to nose, eye to eye. She grunted and twisted, but I was taller and too strong for her, despite her plump arms. I pinched them hard and growled in her face. "And now you will be no more, Ipy! You will be nothing! No one! You will be fortunate to go back to the harem from whence you came!" With a deliberate thrust of my knee into her swollen belly I released her. She dropped to the ground, and I stormed out of the room, calling my servants to me as I left.

Now was the time for vengeance. Yes, let them all burn with my vengeance!

Chapter Nine

The Gift of the Bee-Eater—Nefertiti

"The Great Queen of Amenhotep is dead! The mother of our Pharaoh has passed! Weep and wail, Egypt!" The somber call rang in my ears before I fully woke. Then my young servant girls were around me. Menmet's face was the picture of sadness, although I could hardly believe she felt that way about Tiye's passing. I sat up in my bed and listened as she gave me the full report. The old woman had died last night. Her room had been full of bats, so many that even now the palace servants were beating the animals out of the curtains and drapes where they liked to hide from the sun.

"This is Tadukhipa's work!" I whispered, drawing the blanket up around my face before I began weeping. Since my own mother had died shortly after my birth, Tiye was the only mother I'd known. I wept with my ladies. Finally, I wiped away the tears and said, "Oh, Akhenaten! I must go to him. His heart must be broken."

Menmet shooed the others away and raised her dainty hand in warning. "No, lady. Our Pharaoh does not wish to see anyone. He has hidden himself away in his mother's tomb. He oversees the preparations for her journey to the Otherworld."

"Surely, he would want me by his side. I am the Great Queen!" I said defensively, knowing that I would never go against my husband's explicit instructions. "Did you truly hear this from Akhenaten's servant?"

"Yes, my queen. He has also refused Ipy and the other queens. Except Tadukhipa. She is mourning with him."

"I am sure she is," I said as I climbed out of bed. "No gold today. I will wear colors of mourning, Menmet. As will you all. Put away anything that shines. We will not parade about in gold and silver while our mother, the Mother of Egypt, makes her passage to the Otherworld. Tell the others."

She bowed her head and scooted away to make my wishes known to my personal court. I began to weep again. Although it had been a long time since Tiye had been involved with her son's affairs, I felt alone now. I had no allies here. No one to help me navigate the increasing danger from the Amun priests and those who resented having a Desert Queen as Great Queen of Egypt. I had no time to wallow in sorrow and isolation. I was still Akhenaten's queen. I would go to court, go to the people. I would comfort them in this hour of grief. My head itched, but I postponed shaving it again. Secretly, I mourned my hair. I trusted that Pah knew what she was doing, although for the life of me I could not understand the reason for it. But as she indicated, the stars of the royal family were beginning to fall. I could not allow Smenkhkare, Meritaten, and Tasherit to disappear into the dark night! Although I rarely saw my daughters anymore by order of my own husband, I longed for them with all my being. I would do whatever it took to protect them. I trusted Pah to help me protect them.

Pah must have heard the news. Not fifteen minutes later, her acolyte appeared at my door with a tiny wicker birdcage in her hands. Perched inside a familiar green bird with a hooked beak and nervous eyes. He eyed me suspiciously, as if I'd been the one to stuff him inside his tiny prison. Yes, this was the promised Bee-Eater.

"What does this mean, lady?" one of my maids whispered.

With a quick lie, I replied, "It is a sign of sympathy often exchanged amongst my people. Let us set him here where he can view the courtyard." I walked to the open doors of my balcony and positioned the cage on an empty table. I would set him free before I left. Yes, this was the sign that I must move swiftly. I could no longer postpone my plans. I had to begin my escape in earnest, and I would need help. I dressed quickly in a somber black silk dress with a dull black belt. I paced the floor for a few minutes as I chewed on my nail, a bad habit that I had never been able to shake. To involve another would be to seal their doom if we were caught. It was one thing to put my own life in danger but quite another to place someone I loved in similar peril. It would have to be Menmet! Who else could I go to? Memre was dead, and even if she lived, I doubted she would help me defy her mistress' son.

As I waited for Menmet's return, the bird began to chirp. It was a strange sound to my ears, a sound from my past. How long had it been since I'd allowed myself to think of those days in Timia and Zerzura? After a few more chirps, the bird sang steadily, as if his song could set him free. The city around us wept and mourned for Queen Tiye, but the bird sang his persuasive song. A song of hope. A song of defiance. I listened to his message. Like the Bee-Eater, I would have to keep my hope and avoid the many birds of prey that called Akhenaten's court home. I had to! For Smenkhkare, Tasherit, and Meritaten!

"My queen, will you break your fast now?" Menmet arrived with a small plate of food. I rarely ate this early, but it was kind of her to ask.

"No, Menmet. I will not eat today. I have too much to do. Everyone, leave us." With a nervous eye, Menmet set the plate down and folded her hands in front of her in a poised position to show she was ready to serve me. "Sit, Menmet." She sat on the carpet before me. "No, here. Please." I patted the seat beside me. She sat down, her catlike eyes narrowing slightly, and I said, "I need your help, Menmet. I have to know, can I trust you?" I searched her eyes as if I would see the truth swimming there in the dark depths.

"Always you have trusted Menmet, have you not? I have been your constant companion all these years, my queen. It hurts me to think you must ask this question. How may I serve you, lady queen?" Menmet's soft oriental accent betrayed her origins. It was an echo from her childhood when she lived with her mother far away from the dangerous courts of Thebes and Amarna. I hated her father, but I loved Menmet like a little sister. Sometimes I liked to pretend that she was Paimu, still alive and with me. And despite the fact she was a servant and I could not openly show favoritism, my heart was soft toward her. Would I really put her in this kind of danger? What would I do if she refused me? But she would not refuse. I knew that now.

"Menmet," I whispered, leaning closer to her, "I must leave the palace. I cannot tell you more than that except to say it will be soon."

"No, lady! This is our home. Where will you go?" She covered her open mouth with her hand, and her eyes widened in surprise. "Why must you leave? Has your husband sent you away?"

"No, although I am sure he would if he could. It is not that. You saw the stars fall, didn't you?"

"Yes, but the High One, Nephthys, told us that it was a fortuitous sign. That Pharaoh's glory would be shed upon the earth like the stars falling from on high. Is this not true?"

I shivered at her inclusion of my sister in this conversation. "I cannot speak to that. I only know that I am in danger. My children are in danger. There are shadows moving here in the court, Menmet, shadows that would kill us, kill my children. I must keep them safe. Will you help me?"

"I always help. You are my queen." She touched her fingers to her forehead, making the sign of respect, as she'd seen some do from my homeland. The gesture touched my heart, yet her expression was steady and stern. "What can I do? Where will you go?"

"Because I love you, Menmet, I cannot tell you where I am to go. It would put you in grave danger, and I would rather drown than do such a thing. You are like my own sister."

She looked down at her hands and pouted. "Yes, but you will leave me behind, won't you?"

"I cannot take you with me. It is too dangerous. But if we make the preparations carefully, you will not be harmed. Of that, I am sure."

"I am your servant. I must go with you. No preparations can save me from Pharaoh's wrath, Great Queen."

"Trust me, Menmet. If I were to take you with me, I would place you in more danger than you can imagine."

Her lip trembled, but she said, "Tell me what I must do."

"Please try to understand, Menmet." Her disappointment was apparent, but I told her the truth. I could not risk additional harm to those I loved. For the next few minutes, I whispered my wishes to her, and then she left me to begin her work. I would pray to the Shining Man later. I would pray and hope he listened. It had been so long since I'd seen him. I'd had no dreams, no visions. Surely Akhenaten and I had lost our way. Then I remembered that long-ago dream, the one I would not share with my husband.

He'd been on his throne. A crowd of leopard coats, a larger crowd than any I had seen, appeared before him and then around him. They began chanting and moaning dark phrases, all of which were directed at my husband. Akhenaten began to shout at them, but they would not cease, and they would not listen. Soon, darkness wrapped around his glorious throne and I saw him stand, pushing against that blackness. It did not leave him. As he opened his mouth one last time, a black crow emerged, and he fell down the steps in a heap as the leopard coats crowded around him.

The recollection of the dream filled me with dread. *Oh, my love! If only you would let me help you!* But it was too late now. Too late to fix any of this.

"Great Queen, you have a message." I wiped my eyes with a handkerchief and listened. "Adijah, the ambassador of Grecia, has come at your request. He is in the gallery. Would you like to see him now? Or should I ask him to step into your chambers?"

I thought about that for a moment. Where could we meet? I had to take care not to anger my husband, who already thought me an unfaithful woman. I could not meet with Adijah today, but when? Where? "Tell Adijah to meet me in the vault beneath the palace tomorrow when the sun goes down. I will meet him by the records room." The unknown servant bowed nervously, and I thought for the briefest moment that I saw the hint of a smirk on her face. I certainly wasn't going to call her back and ask her about it. I watched her disappear and heard the bird's sweet song again. No, this must not wait.

Carrying the cage to the balcony, I opened the door to allow the bird his freedom. He had completed his task. He watched me for a few seconds and then suddenly took flight, speeding away from my balcony and our palace. I watched him disappear into the sunshine, feeling nostalgic for home and for freedom. Was it possible that I would be free? And what of my daughters and my son? Would we all die under the weight of my husband's hand?

I did not know, but I refused to wait here to find out.

I'd been waiting too long already.

Chapter Ten

Womb of Spiders—Ipy

A wise woman once told me, "To live in the royal palace is to live in a womb of spiders." I did not understand those words when I first heard them, but the meaning had become very clear to me of late. In the womb of a spider, there is more than one biting mouth that can harm you, more than one spider to kill you. If you want to avoid becoming another casualty of the spider's hunger, you must become a more vicious spider yourself. This epiphany came to me one afternoon while I sat bored in Pharaoh's harem, staring out the window and dreaming of life beyond the palace walls, as we all did from time to time. I was no longer Pharaoh's favorite. He'd cast me off because of some sin my father committed. Even after my father's death, I remained with the other women, a pitiful emblem of the conquests of Amenhotep—or as he preferred to be called now, Akhenaten. I'd once known a life outside this lovely prison, and the memory of that other world stabbed at my heart each day.

Until I began to watch the spider.

She spun and caught her meals without any help from anyone. She mated and killed and cared for her sack of children. I envied her. On more than one occasion, I saved my muse's life from the whisk of a broom. The other women believed me to be simpleminded when I shoved them away. Unlike them, I did not care who wore purple. I cared not about the latest lovers' tricks, the scandals of faraway courts. None of these things intrigued me when I was a girl, yet the spider continued to inspire and amaze me. Even after I woke one morning and found her dead in a tight ball of black legs and torn webs, she inspired me. She'd achieved her task. And I waited for the moment when I could achieve mine.

Eventually, it came. And what a strange thing it was, too. I'd been invited to Akhenaten's court by his Great Queen, and I'd never left.

She too thought me simpleminded, never realizing that inside me was a spider, waiting and watching and spinning. I could not tell what day it was that my web had caught my prey, so slowly had I woven it. At first, Akhenaten barely looked at me, but as he saw that I forgave him and believed that I adored him still, the web tightened. All the while I hated him.

Now, in my womb, I carried my own spider. I would never allow my child to be weak. Never would my child be abandoned. I would teach her—for I was convinced it was a girl-child—that love was an illusion, a spell. It was not real.

I had not always thought so. My father had served the old Pharaoh, but I never liked my father. He reeked of garlic and handled me more than I liked. Also called Ipy, my father had a way of using everything and everyone at his disposal, always for his betterment. I was not sad when he was executed for treason, although my mother mourned for him. No, indeed, I was not. Until I was banished from court, away from Akhenaten forever. Or at least until the arrival of the new Great Queen. When she summoned me, I knew she was in trouble. Why else would she call upon me? I was no one. Amenhotep did not love me, as he had proved. Rarely did he come to see me, and even then only long enough to get me with child, although it had been in his power to call me to him whenever he liked.

I did not dislike the new queen. I hated Tadukhipa much more than I hated Nefertiti. But I loved no one, except for the spider in my belly.

"Lady Ipy. May I come in?" Speaking of spiders, here was another. She stood in the shadows, but I recognized her pretty face. This was Menmet! *Aw, all the pretty spiders are at work today.*

"You may. I seem to be very popular with queens today. Tell me, is it true the old queen is dead? I have heard so, but I don't dare believe it." I sat primly on the couch and waited to see which way the wind would blow with this one. This was the Great Queen Nefertiti's servant. I'd seen her in the court and at other times, always at the queen's beck and call. She did not look me in the face. In fact, I thought she might run away, for she displayed an extraordinary amount of inner struggle. She set her chin and nodded.

"Yes, lady. It is true. We are all to mourn for the next forty days."

"Is that why you have come, Menmet? To express to me the Great Queen's wishes? I know enough to mourn when appropriate. I do not need a mother!" I barked at her. And where were my servants? I wondered absently. Oh, yes, I'd ordered them out after Tadukhipa's visit. Now would be a good time to see them return. Did no one care for me here? I would speak to Amenhotep about this later. I mean, Akhenaten. How strange it was to say that name. As if changing a name would change the man. He would always be what he was, a philanderer. An incompetent leader.

"No, indeed, it is not. The Great Queen does not know I have come here. In fact, she cannot know." I smiled at her answer and patted the cushion beside me. *Oh, yes, here is another spider.*

"You are Heby's daughter, aren't you? Has he sent you here, then?"

She shook her head, her wig bobbing prettily. Finally, she cast those angled eyes upon me, and they were full of tears. "I don't know what to do, Lady Ipy. I know something, something troubling, and the burden is too great. I must tell someone who has our Pharaoh's ear. He must know this, or else I may perish!" I held her hands soothingly, reminding myself not to be too greedy with my response. "I would rather die than return to my father's house or fall under the weight of my Pharaoh Akhenaten's anger!"

"Come now, Menmet. Calm yourself, dear. I can see you have come to me with troubling news. I will surely speak to Pharaoh on your behalf. You have no need to worry. Tell me, what is in your heart?" I made my voice soft and sweet, just as I did with Amenhotep.

"I would never speak against my lady queen, but I know I will die if I do not. She doesn't know what she is doing. I think she is riddled with grief because of the queen mother's passing. That must be it. Yes, that is it." She wept now and sat in a blubbering heap beside me. *How long must I endure this? Oh, yes, be patient, little spider.*

"So, you have no wish to tell me what you came to tell me, then? You may leave if you like, Menmet, without worry that I would betray your concerns. Please know that I am here whenever you need me." I hugged her even though I hated to do so. This kind of contact did not come naturally to me, but I knew it soothed others. This woman was a fountain of information, and this spider would benefit from that information. I stroked her wig and patted her shoulder, ready for there to be more distance between us.

"No, I must tell you. I came to you because I know something of your past, lady. I too have a father who has fallen out of favor with Pharaoh. I am content to serve the Great Queen, but I cannot help but worry for my sister and myself if the Great Queen succeeds in her plan."

"Oh, Menmet. What a heavy burden for such slender shoulders! I cannot believe our Great Queen would put you in such a delicate position. It must be grief, yes, that must be it. And yes, you and I have much in common, but we need not be defined by our fathers. We are our own women, called into the service of our great Pharaoh Akhenaten. Let us serve him with all our hearts, even our bodies if we must."

She nodded and whispered, "The queen makes plans to leave, Lady Ipy. She will not tell me when and where, but she will leave us. How can this be? What do I do?"

I squeezed her hands and mimicked her sad face. "Serve the Great Queen. Be her friend, as you have always been. I will find out the truth. Rest assured, all will be well, Menmet." I rose from the couch, anxious for this meeting to end. Menmet was ready to be rid of me, having done what she came to do. What a shameful thing! I wondered why she would betray her queen in such a way! She would never serve in my court. This was further proof that all women were spiders.

"And you will speak for me, Lady Ipy? You will not let me die in the flames?" Her shimmering black eyes searched mine, and I gave her a sympathetic, solemn look.

"You can trust me. I will not abandon you. Go now and do your mistress' bidding. Keep your face dry and let no one know what you have told me. I will speak to my husband, I mean, Pharaoh."

No, I would never trust her, nor would I help her. In fact, as soon as she left me, I planned to break Akhenaten's ban on solitude. He would want to know this, and I should be the one to tell him! With an awkward glance over her shoulder, Menmet disappeared into the shadowy corridor, and I turned to my mirror.

What does one wear when overthrowing a queen?

Chapter Eleven

The Broken Man—Pah

Walking at a steady pace, I moved through the Green Temple. I kept my eyes on the distant statue of Isis, the center of all this attention. Today was a day of mourning in the city. Queen Tiye's body had been removed this morning and taken to the priests for her preparations for her journey. Or so the Egyptians believed. Despite the overwhelming sadness that hovered over everything, rumors of my betrayal flitted about all of Akhenaten's city. As sheltered as they were, the priestesses were not immune to the gossip. Ignoring their stares, pretending that all was well, I carried an armful of sweet flowers to the image of Isis in honor of the late queen. These were rare yellow blooms, expensive and hard to find in the city. It was well known that I grew them with my own hands on my balcony from seeds. What most didn't know was that those seeds had been a present from Adijah a few years ago. When I pushed the seeds down into the soil, I had visions of faraway Grecia, but I knew full well I would never see that fair land.

I liked Adijah, and that was not something I could say about most people. Perhaps that was why I excelled in my role as priestess. I had to do very little speaking, and when I did, those who listened hung on my every word. Yes, I liked Adijah. He looked very much like a foreigner compared to those around us, but I supposed I did too. He had trustworthy eyes, and I did trust him. What other choice did we have now? Allies were few and far between in Akhenaten's court.

The whispers of the acolytes rose as I approached the towering image of Isis.

"This is strange indeed for the high priestess to arrive unannounced," I heard them say. "Something must be amiss! Can the rumors be true?"

With a wave of my hand, I dismissed them. Arranging the flowers at Isis' feet, I knelt as the last of the attending priestesses left the room.

The High One's worship was sacred and not to be witnessed by anyone. Only one priestess lingered—Maza was her name. Her dark skin looked otherworldly and bright compared to the soft yellow gown she wore. Yes, Maza would be the one who would rule this place after me. I stared at her unflinchingly as she slowly closed the door behind her. Like me, she had likely seen our entwined fates in the fire and the water, but she was not yet the ruler of this place. Not yet. But soon.

I did not waste time wallowing at the statue's feet. The old queen was dead, and it was the current queen and my sister who needed my help. What prayer could I offer for Tiye, the tiny Red Lands woman who had ruled Egypt with an iron fist until she lost her mind—and her power over her son? I quickly set about my task, searching through the many baskets that lay at the goddess' feet. Inside one of them, I would find what I was looking for. Surely he had not let me down. Not this time. After plundering through a dozen offerings of fruits, meats, and breads, I found my prize. Yes, here it was!

It was a small piece of papyrus hidden under an orange. If I'd been paying closer attention, I would have recognized the Grecian flowers, the same kind as the ones I'd offered, tucked in the corner. No matter now. I found it! Clutching it in my hand, I fell before the statue and began to sing a song of mourning as I'd been taught.

Eyes watched me now. The awareness made my skin crawl, and I could feel those eyes, wondering, watching, observing my every move. I slid the small papyrus fragment into the bosom of my gown as I waved my arms about and bowed before the statue again and again. Yes, I heard the shuffling of sandals not far behind me. It could only be Maza, for no one else dared to enter this holy place unsummoned. I pretended that I did not notice her presence, continuing until my knees ached and my arms grew weary. Finally, I took some of the flowers and tossed them into the sacred fire. They burned quickly, leaving nothing but soot behind. Such a shame to burn such beauty. It had been my intention to gaze into the fire before I returned to my apartments to prepare, but I could not, not while my watcher hung nearby. Instead, I burned another handful of the flowers and shut my eyes against whatever I might see.

That was a mistake, for Maza was close enough to see for herself what was in the fire. I heard her gasp, and I spun about to meet her face to face. But it was not Maza who looked into the fire. It was my servant and student, Shepshet.

"Shepshet! What are you doing here? You know that you cannot be here."

Her eyes were wide and her mouth open in surprise still. She could not shake her gaze from the fire, and instead sank to her knees and began to weep. "Oh, lady! What have I seen? What have I seen?"

I fell down beside her and cupped her face with my hands, forcing her to break her fiery vision. "You have seen nothing, Shepshet! Nothing!"

She shook her head slowly, miserably, as tears slid down her cheeks. What had she seen? "I did see. I saw you die, Nephthys."

"No, Shepshet. Listen to me. Look at me. Look into my eyes. Do not stare into the fire again." Finally, she did as I asked, her body limp, her emotions clearly raw and ragged. At least one person would mourn my leaving this world. Better that than the thousands of Egyptians who only pretended to grieve for the loss of Queen Tiye. For the past twenty-four hours, they had paraded in and out of our courtyards, making sure they were seen by anyone who cared to look. Each hoped that word would travel back to Pharaoh Amenhotep, as if he would be impressed by their devotion. These Egyptians thought of nothing but politics. They did not impress me with their displays of mourning—ashes on their bald heads, arms free of gold. "You have seen nothing but what must be. You cannot prevent this. And you must not."

"But..."

"No, Shepshet. I do not wish for you to share my fate. Do not tell anyone what you have seen. You must obey me in this. I cannot meet whatever lies before me knowing you are in danger. It would be too much to bear. And remember, we are all in her hands." I glanced up at the statue, and Shepshet's fearful eyes followed mine. Then she clung to me and sobbed. I allowed myself to feel self-pity for a few seconds but not for too long. I could not afford to lose faith now. I had to continue on if I wanted to make peace with Paimu and see Alexio once again. Oh, to step on the soft grass of Timia again, to see the ones I had loved all those years ago.

And when did you leave this world, my love? How is it that I didn't sense your passing?

"You must leave now, Shepshet. I must continue with my ministrations, but I will return to my apartments soon." We rose together, and I hugged her one last time. "Now, do not let anyone see your tears. Pull your veil down. And Shepshet..."

"Yes?"

"See that no one else comes in. I want to be alone for a while."

"Yes, lady." She did as I asked, pulling the veil over her face and quietly exiting the room. I watched the door close and quickly walked behind the statue. Now I was truly alone. I dug the papyrus out of my dress. Looking around one last time, I unrolled it with shaking fingers and stared at the painted emblems.

There were three. But that was all that was needed. I touched the script with my fingers as if I could make the emblems speak to me. The first was simple enough, the sign of the Meshwesh. The careful squiggles represented the falcon, the symbol of our people, only it was upside down. Next to it was an unusual image, the horns of a bull. I stared at the last picture—the broken man, his arms and legs detached from his body.

My uncle's message was clear. The falcon's day had ended. Horemheb left Egypt with Kames by his side, as I had instructed.

Somehow, Ayn's son would be crucial for the survival of the Meshwesh. He was the bull, as his name suggested.

I stared at the broken man. It could only mean that Pharaoh's judgment was against me. Horemheb would know this. Until recent years he had been one of Amenhotep's favorites, and even now, his tenuous connections kept him abreast of the ebb and flow of Pharaoh's mood. Apparently, it now flowed against me. He had already purposed in his heart to tear me asunder. He was unable to deliver his rage upon Nefret, so it would fall upon me.

I would be the broken man.

Chapter Twelve

Hidden Places—Nefertiti

Sleep struggled with me, but eventually, I grasped it, and quiet darkness took me. But it didn't stay dark for long. A glow surrounded me, and my skin tingled with warmth. I was floating, and in that strange levitation, there was peace and stillness. Yes, this was where I wanted to be. Let me stay here a little while. Away from my troubles and despair!

Now I was falling. Terror seized me as I stretched out my hands. I struggled to find something I could use to break my fall, but it continued, seemingly endless. I felt as if time stood still as I whipped around, head over feet again and again. The motion threatened to make me sick as I spun faster with each passing moment. I screamed for what felt like a lifetime, but no one heard me, nothing happened, and eventually my voice failed me. Yet I continued to fall. I forced my eyes shut and hugged myself as I waited for the impending crash. Surely I would die.

Then I wasn't falling but standing in the Red Lands, the sand warm beneath my feet. I gasped in surprise because I was not alone. The Shining Man stood beside me. As always, his face was obscured by the light that surrounded him—no, he was the source of the light. He watched me but said nothing at first, and I felt uneasy under his gaze.

What could I say? What could I do but wait to hear what he would say? Would he impart to me another dream? Another vision for the future? And why should he trust me with a new vision, seeing that my husband and I had failed so miserably with the dream he'd given me? No, I was not worthy of being here. Surely this was a mistake.

"What makes one man or woman worthier than another?"

I couldn't hide my surprise. He could read my mind!

"I do not know," I began hesitantly. "But I am sure you do, sir."

Although I could not see his face, I could *feel* him smile. It gave me the confidence to continue standing in his presence, for without it I am sure I would have perished.

"Worthiness is a human measurement. Worthiness is man's attempt at reasoning with the workings of the divine." His words both comforted and disturbed me. *Why then do men try to please the gods?* I thought, forgetting that he could read my thoughts. I quickly repented of the question, but before I could sort out my many emotions, he touched my shoulder with a firm grip. At that moment, everything became clear to me. Who he was, who I was, where we were, and where I would go next. I knew that far from failing him, failing the vision, Amenhotep and I had *accomplished* his desires. The knowledge of that brought me much peace—peace of a kind I had not known in my waking life. No matter what happened, no matter what I lost or who I lost, all would be well. In fact, as I woke, I heard him speak those words to my heart.

All will be well...

As I opened my eyes and exited the dream world, the knowledge I had so richly enjoyed fluttered away from me. It flew away on invisible wings, vanishing on the rays of the approaching dawn. It seemed like I had been there only a moment, but apparently, I'd slept soundly through the night. Morning was arriving. As I had when I fell, I grasped the air around me as if the knowledge were a tangible thing to be possessed. It was not. I could remember nothing except the Shining Man's words.

All will be well. Strangely, it was enough. I rose from my bed quickly to dress. I had taken to sleeping alone now. I did not need to worry that Amenhotep would discover the change in my hairstyle. He had not come to my bed in nearly a season. But if I was to prevent my servants from knowing I had shaved my head, I must be alone. I had to admit I missed Menmet's nighttime chatter. She had always been so entertaining. I pulled on my morning wig and a loose robe and opened the outer door to my sleeping chamber. To my surprise there was no one about. This had never happened before, and it was a strange thing indeed.

With my heart pounding, I examined this new development. What could possibly have occurred? Reality struck me. Queen Tiye was dead, along with the last of her influence and presumably also mine. Or maybe this was a sign that Menmet had deceived me. Soon the palace guards would set upon me and take me before my husband.

"Lady? I did not hear you rise. Are you hungry? Won't you take some food, my queen?"

"Where is Menmet?" I asked the girl.

She stammered, "I do not know. I woke to an empty room, lady." She stood at attention and glanced around nervously. Even this inexperienced girl knew all was not right here. Well, I wasn't one to cower because a few servants had left me for higher ground. *All the more reason to leave as soon as possible. Do not let her betray me! Let me have my daughters and my son, and I will ask for nothing more!*

"What is your name?"

"Yerye, Great Queen."

"Yerye, I am hungry. Please bring me a tray to the balcony. After my devotion to the Aten, I will take some food. Then you may help me dress."

"Oh, yes, lady!" She smiled with great delight, immediately forgetting the strange predicament we found ourselves in. I took some comfort in her obliviousness. She waited as I offered my worship to the Aten—I would need his favor if my plan was to succeed.

I took a few bites of food and said as absently as I could, "Yerye, after I dress, I want you to send the steward to fetch my daughters for me. They are at the White Palace."

"Oh, no, lady. They are not. They are here." She blinked as she set the blue pitcher down on the table beside me.

I gripped her wrist as quickly as a cobra striking his prey. "Tell me where you saw them! Have they been harmed?"

She winced in surprise and pain but did not pull away from me. Instead, she fell on her knees and said, "They seemed healthy, lady queen. I did not speak with them, for I am just a servant." I released her wrist and waited to hear more. "I saw them playing in the Great Hallway with Lady Ipy and her dogs. I can fetch them now if you like." As she spoke, my anger rose. How dare Ipy reach for my daughters! Yes, I must go tonight! Adijah must help me, as Pah promised he would.

"Yes, that will be fine. Only don't bring them here. I will go to my gardens. You can bring them to me there, Yerye."

"Very well, Great Queen." I heard the doors to my chambers open and close, but I did not turn my head. I kept my eyes on the horizon while I reclined on my balcony. It would not do to quiver like a coward before my husband's guards, if indeed they were the ones who were barging in on me.

"Great Queen, I had hoped to return before you woke. Forgive Menmet for not being here to help you dress as I have always done."

Angrily I launched from my couch and swung my gown back as I stepped toward her. As petite as she was, I towered over her, and as angry as I was, I didn't mind reminding her of my advantage. I wanted to strike her in the face for her betrayal, for I was sure she had betrayed me, but before my hand could fulfill my wishes, my daughters rushed onto the balcony and encircled my waist with their arms.

"Mother!" Meritaten kissed my cheek and hugged me close, closer than she had in a long time. I kissed her back and rubbed her chin as I did when I greeted her. When she was a babe, it was the only thing that kept her from crying. Pharaoh had wet nurses and servants aplenty for our children, but only I could care for my daughter, my own Meritaten. She would have no other until she got older and decided she no longer needed a mother. But perhaps I was being unkind. Like all the other women in her father's court, including me, she had little to say about where she went and who she saw. Meritaten had her father's sculpted mouth but my green eyes. She had my height, and I believed she'd grown since last I saw her, but I did not say so. She was a sensitive girl who was prone to be upset about the slightest perceived offense. In that she reminded me of Pah and at times Sitamen, who preferred solitude over court life.

Tasherit came next. She was Tiye made over with her big dark eyes and flat feet. Would she ever grow? I could not tell, but I always told her that she had. I sat again so I could scoop her into my arms. Menmet beamed behind them, and I immediately felt sorry for my black thoughts toward her. "Thank you, Menmet. That will be all." She winked at me and stepped back, making the sign of respect as she did. I noticed that my chambers were now full of servants, but most of them I did not know. Something was mightily wrong here, but at least I saw my daughters.

"Mother, what a sad time. Our grandmother has died. Will you die also, my mother?" Tasherit's young voice broke my heart.

"Someday we all will leave this world for the next, but I promise you that the Otherworld is a wonderful place. Even now, your grandmother, the Great Queen Tiye, is walking the shores with your grandfather Amenhotep."

I noticed that Meritaten sighed a great deal as Tasherit and I spoke. She was obviously unhappy and wanted me to know it. Yes, I had been away from my daughters for too long. How foolish I'd been! This was real love.

"Why do you tell her these tales, mother? We both know that not all stories have a happy ending."

So that's it, then. Meritaten has heard the news. Smenkhkare will marry Ipy's daughter. If only she understood the much greater danger that faced us all. And how could I tell her that we would leave her father's kingdom like bandits in the night? This I could not do.

"Tasherit? Go to Mother's ivory table, the one by my bed. Open the middle drawer. I think you will find a treasure there. It is something that flies."

She showed a gap-toothed smile. "If I find it and bring it back to you, will you tell me a story?" And she quickly added, "And can I keep my treasure?"

I laughed at her enthusiasm. Of all my children, Tasherit loved my stories—and my treasures—best. "Why, yes! Now go, my smart girl!" She took off running, her bare feet slapping on the floor. She was a tiny thing. I turned to Meritaten and said, "What is on your heart, my daughter? You can speak freely to me."

"There is nowhere free here." Meritaten crossed her arms and stared out across the city to the sands beyond. After a minute, she added, "I used to hate you, Mother. I don't now, but I used to."

"Why?" I asked, surprised by her admission. "Have I wronged you in some way?"

"No, it is not that." She sighed, turned her back to the railing, and tapped her fingers on the carved wood. "I thought you did not love us. I remember those times when my father would wave you to his side, and you would leave us. We cried for you, but you never came. Sometimes for weeks. I would think, how can any mother leave their child for such a long time? Even if her husband is the great Pharaoh? But that was before—before I knew what love was myself."

"Before you knew you loved Smenkhkare?"

"You know?"

"Of course, I know. I am his mother too."

When I said nothing else, she added, "And you don't approve?"

"I never had the opportunity to approve or disapprove. My son told me of his intentions after it was too late for me to intervene. I cannot go against the wishes of the Pharaoh. And sadly, even if Smenkhkare had consulted me earlier, I am not sure it would have availed much."

Suddenly Meritaten threw herself in my lap and wept loudly. The servants paused and whispered, but no one dared to invade our privacy. Except for Menmet, who stood nearby. I waved her back and stroked Meritaten's arm.

"There now, sweet daughter. All will be well." *Ah, yes. Those words did bring comfort to us, didn't they?* "You have to trust fate. If it is meant to be, it will happen."

"How can that be? He is to marry that awful girl! He doesn't want to—can't you help us? Don't you understand how it feels?" She looked up at me, her pretty face filled with deep emotion.

"I wish it were that easy. You can't give up hope, Meritaten. You must keep hope."

She pushed me away and sobbed in the corner of the balcony. "And that is your advice? Keep hope? I will not stand idly by and watch him marry her!"

I rushed to her side. "Hush now, daughter. You cannot lose control like this. It will not do you any good. Believe me, I know."

She spun around, her eyes now streaked with makeup, her lip quivering. "How has that worked for you, Mother? Has silently waiting like a dutiful wife helped you at all? There is open talk that Pharaoh will make Ipy Great Queen. Do you know what that means? We will all be ruined! And you do nothing? By the gods! She wears your crown, Mother!"

She shouted at me now, but I gripped her hands and said in a low whisper, "There are spies here, Meritaten!" I stared her down to demonstrate the danger. When she stilled for a moment, I continued, "No one here is my friend. Keep your voice down. I will help you as much as I can, but if you do not keep silent, I cannot help you at all. What now would you have me do? Throw a tantrum as you have done? And whose lap can I fall into? Let Ipy parade around in whatever crown she likes. I face more dangerous things than the loss of a crown or a few baubles."

She snatched her hands away and said in a vicious whisper, "Yes! Yes, you do."

Without waiting for my leave, Meritaten stormed out of my chambers, pushing past even Tasherit who had appeared with the promised treasure in her hands. My younger daughter's eyes were full of fear and worry. She glanced from me to Meritaten's vanishing figure. I held out my arms to her, but I could see the conflict on her face. She'd been with her sister all these months. Leaving the paper bird on a stick on my table, she left me and ran out. "Meritaten! Wait for me!" she called as she vanished from my view.

I nearly collapsed into my chair. Then I caught a glimpse of Menmet as she slipped behind the curtain. I saw a smile on her face.

Chapter Thirteen

The Bones of Ayn—Tadukhipa

From the comfort of my bed, I watched the young man put on his clothes, fully appreciating his perfect physique. It was true that looking at him pleased me, but it was an empty pleasure, not like what I had felt in the arms of Inhapi. Men were not capable of love. I had never experienced that kind of love or witnessed it. All men were unfaithful. They were like animals, really, useful for only one thing, or perhaps two, depending on the man. I spun the sweet-smelling rose next to my nose as the young man returned to my bed to steal another kiss before leaving, but I did not give him one. "No more today, Seker. You must earn your next kiss."

He smiled at me and said, "Haven't I done that, my queen? What can I do now to please you? Just name your desire, for it pleases me to please you."

I had no doubt that he meant it, even though I was old enough to be his mother—or at least his much older sister. Such stupidity in those exquisite eyes, but I liked a stupid man. I had no worries that Seker plotted against me, and I knew he would never incite me to overthrow my husband.

The downside was he had no idea that I was on the verge of losing my claim to the high queenship, which would surely become available soon, as soon as Amenhotep mustered up the courage to execute the Desert Queen. That high place would go to Ipy. Once she became the next Great Queen, she would have complete control over us all. That could not be borne! How cruel to see my plan backfire on me so! After hearing of the Desert Queen's treasonous affair with Aperel, Amenhotep was supposed to put her away or burn her, not raise the fat Ipy to new heights. As always, Pharaoh was unpredictable. And weak when it came to Nefertiti.

"Go to the Great Queen and command her attend me. Tell her I wish to see her in my chambers in one hour." If I could not work with Ipy, I might be able to entice Nefertiti to help me rid us both of her nasty presence.

His smile vanished, and he stammered stupidly, "I cannot command the Great Queen, but I'll be happy to relay your request to her."

I slapped his face with the rose, and a thorn left a long scratch across his cheek and cleft chin. "Get out and don't return," I shouted. Blood poured from the scratch, and he held his hand to his face. I rolled over on my back and ignored him as he stomped away to tend to his wound and obey my command. Yes, he brought me pleasure from time to time, but he had no courage. Aggravated by his insubordination, I rolled out of bed and poured myself some water.

Hours later, I was still mulling over my situation, and I began to regret my hastiness. Seker did not return—in this, he obeyed me—and I had too much pride to send for him so soon. But I regretted sending him away. He risked his life night after night crawling into my bed. That was proof of his courage, wasn't it? What else did I want? For him to throw himself into the Burning Bull? I shivered, thinking of Ramose and Sitamen, burning and twisting together in death. It had been a horror to witness.

"Queen Tadukhipa, you have a visitor."

"Yes? Who is it?" Perhaps it was Seker returning to beg my forgiveness!

"It is the Great Queen, Neferneferuaten Nefertiti." My servant bowed her head and waited for me to command her. This was an interesting turn of events, wasn't it? I never thought I would see the day when the Desert Queen darkened my doorway. Sailing past the bowed servant, I entered my main chamber to find my sister-queen waiting for me. She'd not waited for me to invite her to sit. She sat already—and in my chair.

"Queen Nefertiti? To what do I owe this rare pleasure?"

"Leave us," she said to my retinue of slaves and servants. They did not hesitate to obey her, but they went only as far as the antechamber. Obediently they closed the door and left us alone. Had we ever been alone before? And where were her servants? Didn't they fear for her safety? How foolish to trust me!

"State your business, *Great Queen*," I said sarcastically. "Have you come for my help with Ipy? I can tell you from personal experience that she is an unpleasant sort of woman and not moved by common sense. I am afraid you are too late to overthrow her. You should have asked me before you invited her here."

She did not hesitate to speak, but she did not address my comments at all. "I know it was you who caused the death of Queen Tiye." I did not deny it, and she kept talking. "I know it was you who spread the rumors that the Master of Horse and I met privately. That I was involved with him in an illicit manner."

I did not deny that either. A small smile crept across my face. "And what of it?" Did she want me to deny it? I was happy that she recognized my handiwork, but I was in no mood to play games with a pouting queen—one who was destined for banishment or worse.

"Be sure your own sins will find you, Tadukhipa. Those who do evil always find their deeds revisited on them."

Unimpressed with her scolding, I sat in a smaller chair at the square table between us. This table and the elegant chair that the queen claimed for herself had been gifts from my father, a few of my wedding gifts. Each piece served as a reminder of who I was and the blood I came from. Royal blood. I used to love looking at it, running my fingers in the grooves, reading again and again the story of the Hittites that was scripted in the panels. So strong we were, and absolutely ruthless when necessary. But even though those things were treasures to me, what rested in the box between us was the most interesting thing in the room. I was sure Queen Nefertiti would want to see it. I just had to wait for the right moment! I rubbed my finger over the top of the box. It was a plain thing but a fitting home for what lay inside it.

"Tell me, Great Queen. Did you come all this way to tell me a story about virtue and morality? I hear you are very good at telling stories, but I am no child and have no time to hear one. I have many things to do today."

She gave me a lovely smile, and immediately I sensed the danger. She said sweetly, "Indulge me, my sister. This will not take long. I think this story will interest you a great deal, probably more than any other you have heard lately. It is the story of an evil witch who cast a spell on her husband. While he was under her spell, he made many poor decisions. He did many things he regretted. But one day, a little bird came to him and whispered words in his ear. Those words were magic words, and they broke the spell of the witch. His evil wife had no more power over him. The husband realized his mistake and immediately corrected it. He cast out the witch into the darkness and called her wife no more."

I leaned forward and stared at her in disbelief. "Is this supposed to frighten me? It's no wonder that Ipy climbs so high. I despise game-playing. Tell me what is on your mind and be done with it." My skin crawled in anticipation of what she would tell me.

"Very well. Seker, your most recent lover, is now before the king. He is blubbering like an infant and has fully confessed to his crimes. He will die, just as innocent Aperel died. Except Aperel never accused me or confessed to the accusation, for it was only that. I have never taken another man to my bed. Seker says he has been your lover for some time."

Springing to my feet, I beat the table with my fist. "You lie!"

She smiled even wider. "I have it on good authority, Tadukhipa. It is a shame, though. He was so young and inexperienced. I am sure there was much you could have taught him if given a chance."

I stared at her, hardly believing what she said. It couldn't be true! Having delivered her hateful words to my face, she acted as if she would leave me.

"No! Wait, Great Queen." It was my turn to smile now, my turn to give her a gift. "Since you were kind enough to visit me today and deliver this news personally, it is only fair that I give you something."

Nefertiti's back straightened, and she watched me as I opened the box. I pulled back the black cloth that covered my treasure. How long I had been waiting to show this to her! I revealed the bones and plucked out the necklace I'd stashed with them. She should recognize it. I tossed the thing in her lap and stepped back, waiting to see how she liked her present.

The leather and turquoise necklace was unique but obviously not as finely made as anything Egyptian. Just another desert treasure not worth the time it took to make. She gingerly picked it up from her lap. I noticed that she wore black today again, and like an undignified foreign queen, she wore no gold or jewels. Did she believe Tiye would have done the same for her? Still in mourning for the crazy old woman, I supposed, and how much more she would mourn now. She rubbed the pendant and looked at the bones. I picked up the skull and rolled it around in my hands before offering it to her. "Do you recognize her? She is quite a bit thinner now." I laughed at my own joke, but it yielded no response from her.

She slid the necklace around her neck and rose from my favorite chair. "Well? How do you like my gift?" I asked her. She did not accept the skull, and I tired of holding it. I bounced the gaping thing back in its box and smiled innocently, satisfied that my arrow had hit the mark. If she had not thought me evil before, she would certainly think me so now. "Answer me. I am not used to being ignored."

"You are an evil woman. And not just evil but mad as well. I have long made peace with Ayn's passing, but you must live with your lover's death today. That is enough."

I screamed with fury and shoved her as hard as I could. Nefertiti fell on her backside but did not stay down long. She raced across the room, I thought to escape me. But instead, she charged for the long golden spear on the wall. With surprising strength, she pulled it down and hefted it like a warrior. I firmly believed she would drill a hole in me if she could.

I picked up a small bust of Amenhotep and pitched it at her. It landed at her feet, and the enamel coating cracked but did not break. A few more inches and it would have struck her. She poked at me with the spear as I searched for a weapon. I tossed a platter at her, which she dodged, but soon I spotted what I'd been looking for. The long blade stood in the corner. It was a blade like those used by a queen's guard, left here for some reason just yesterday. Such a strange thing to see because I already possessed many ceremonial weapons, most of which had been given to me by my father and uncle. Perhaps my husband hoped I'd run myself through with the guard's sword so he could finally be rid of me. That I would never do. If he wanted me to die, he would have to see to it himself. And if Seker betrayed me, Amenhotep might very well do it after all.

I had no training with a sword, no skill with a blade, yet my black anger would not allow me to relent.

"You are making a mistake, Tadukhipa. Another mistake."

I sliced at her, but her spear kept me at a safe distance. She was toying with me now. "I hate you! I hate you!" I screamed at her.

"Stop this madness!" she screamed back, but I noticed she did not lower her own weapon. Suddenly the doors of the chamber opened, and the servants rushed in. They cried out, at what I did not know. Perhaps they were warning us to stop. My mind was full of angry bees, and I could barely hear anything over their buzzing. Then the cries rose like a strange tide, from the surrounding palace and the city below. I lowered my sword and beheld Mure's face.

"What is it?"

"Pharaoh is dead, mistress! Our sovereign is dead!" She fell to her knees and began weeping, as did the others. They hardly seemed to notice that I held a sword and Nefertiti a spear.

"What will become of us? What will become of us?" another cried out in agony.

I dropped my sword and fell into my chair. I could not help but scream. I clawed at my arms and beat my chest with my fists. "No! This cannot be true! Amenhotep! Husband!" I said again, pushing my servants away. Through my tears, I saw Nefertiti drop the spear, and it clanged on the marble floor. Without another word or a hint of emotion, she departed quickly.

My mind screamed, "Now is the time! Kill her now!" but my heart would not allow me to act. It was broken. All my love had been squeezed from it. All my hope.

It was at that moment that I realized the agonizing truth. I had loved Amenhotep from the first day I saw him to this day. I *had* loved him utterly and completely. And like Inhapi, he was gone.

I had nothing else to live for.

Chapter Fourteen

Tasherit cried herself to sleep after our brief visit with Mother. The poor girl cried so hard she made herself physically sick. My little sister begged me to go back and apologize to our mother for leaving so abruptly, but I would not. I told her to go back herself if she wanted to, that I would not hold it against her, but she would not leave me. That both comforted me and filled my heart with guilt. Eventually, Tasherit stopped asking me to return to Mother and closed her eyes. Once her breathing settled, she succumbed to sleep, and I left her for a little while. I would never leave her for too long. All we had was each other. But it was difficult to find time for myself, so I selfishly stole it whenever I could.

It was only a matter of time before my sister and I were shipped back to the White Palace, and I wanted to visit the stables again. These were far superior to ours. My father kept his finest breeds at his palace, and some were protected by armed guards since they were rare and very costly. I especially loved the black chariot horses, although they were smaller than the war horses. Smenkhkare loved his war horses. Not me. I would trade any of my treasures for a pair of these chariot horses, and these two were powerful animals and demonstrated great loyalty to one another. Loyalty. It was such a rare thing.

My servant, Sarai, whom I'd named Lurker because of her tall frame and saggy dark eyes, stayed in the palace after first defying my commands several times. It wasn't until I threatened to thrash her that she obeyed me. Sarai was so slow that it wasn't really difficult to leave her behind, but she was very persistent. She did not speak much, and that at least was something. Tasherit talked nonstop from the time she woke up until her head hit the pillow at night, so Sarai's quiet presence did not irritate me often. I craved quiet.

I found the horses quite easily in the closest set of stables. As if they remembered I always had treats in my pocket, they began to stamp and snort at the sight of me.

"Hail, Raja and Kamara. Yes, I have something for you."

Despite my current sadness and worry, the animals pulled a smile out of me. I held out some sugar cubes and let them take turns licking my palms. Once they had their snacks, I rubbed their noses lovingly. I wondered what it would be like to ride a chariot horse into battle. Last year during our visit here, Aperel had let me sit atop one. Of course, I was not allowed to ride freely, not without his hand holding the reins. He'd warned me that these were too powerful for a young girl to master. But that minor encounter with the horses did not satisfy me.

Aperel had been a nice man, and I'd found him to be intelligent. And he obviously held great affection for the animals in his care. I had been surprised to learn he was a traitor. Like everyone else, I'd heard the rumors about him and my mother, but unlike Smenkhkare, I did not believe them to be true. Anyone with brains knew Mother had eyes for no one except our father. And what would have been so wrong if she had loved another? In the past few years Father had become a distant man, pushing away all those he once cherished, including his children. I could not explain this change in him, and it was easier to just blame Mother. She should have tried harder to keep his love intact. For if he had not fallen out of love with her, we would all be happy still.

Surely that was her fault.

"Yes, Raja. You are a greedy one, aren't you?" The dark horse nudged my pocket, and I gave him my last treat. Kamara snorted in offense, but I had nothing else to give. "Too bad, handsome. You should have been more persistent. Now your brother has taken it all." I smiled again as Raja's tongue searched my palm for his prize. He flicked his ears at me with pleasure as Kamara turned his head away for a moment. He did not trust me now that he knew I had favored his brother.

Ah, you'd better get used to that. Life is not fair, and neither are the gods and goddesses who so cruelly rule us all.

"I knew I would find you here, Meri-meri."

I didn't turn around. "Nobody calls me that anymore. That's a childhood name, a name I would like to leave behind." The truth was, our father had called me that, back when he loved me still. I couldn't bear to look at Smenkhkare. Not without crying like a baby. I reached for a brush from a nearby rack and began carefully stroking Raja's coat. He did not need it, but I needed something to do with my hands. I had never been allowed to perform this task myself, but I had watched the horse masters enough times to know how it was done. You started at the animal's back and swept the brush down in even strokes. It wasn't hard. And if I could brush Tasherit's hair, this would be an easy job. Raja seemed to enjoy the treatment, even if it was administered by inexperienced hands. He shivered in appreciation and nuzzled me repeatedly. I said softly, "I don't want to see you, brother. There is nothing else to say."

"Why call me 'brother'? You know we are more than that. But I have something to say to you. Please, Meritaten, listen to me."

With tears stinging my eyes, I answered him, "Then say what you have to if it helps you. I will not stop you. You are co-regent now, aren't you? It is your right to speak to whomever you choose. Tell me, have you visited our sister yet? Did she welcome you with a flower wreath and some pomegranates?"

"Why do you say such things? And you should not blame Ankhesenamun. This was not her idea. She is a child, Meritaten, and must obey. May I remind you this was a marriage I did not want?"

"I see you are broken up about it." I turned my back to him again and continued brushing Raja's silky coat.

"You misunderstand me, Meri-meri. I will not accept her. I intend to refuse the marriage. It is my right as co-regent."

His words made me stop in mid-brush. With a glance over my shoulder, I asked, "How do you intend to defy our father? You know you can't do that. If Father said it, it is the law."

"I have a plan." He touched my shoulder, and it burned my skin. I could not help but feel hope rise in me, just as Mother had predicted.

Hope, Meritaten. You must keep hope.

"What is your plan?" I whispered as I fought the urge to abandon all and fall into his arms.

"Kames. He will help us, I am sure of it. As the eldest brother, he must marry first."

"And what if he has no mind to marry? What then?"

"If he must be compelled to take our sister as wife, then I will compel him to do it. It is true. I have consulted my scribes, and they tell me this is how it is always done in Pharaoh's family. Pharaoh may choose whomever he likes for co-regent, but his sons must be afforded marriage according to their ages. Kames must marry first. At the very least, we will have more time to find another way." Pulling himself up to his full height he added, "And if I must, I will die before I marry Ankhesenamun. You are my true love, Meritaten. It is only you I love. I want no other wives, and no other shall take your place, my love. You are everything."

I flung my arms around his neck and hugged him with the weight of my body. I sobbed in relief. "I love you too, Smenkhkare. You are my life and breath! If I had to choose from all the men in all the world, I would choose you. Always! There is no one but you for me." I laid my head upon his chest as he stroked my hair.

Let this moment be for always. Yes, let it be for always!

"Let them try to separate us!" he said in a savage whisper. "And no matter what, we will be together. Even if we must perish like Ramose and Sitamen."

I shivered to hear him say that, but I agreed with all my heart.

Then all the world erupted into screams, as if they had heard our words to one another. Screams and cries erupted from the palace and swept across the complex. People ran outside and tossed heaps of sand upon their heads.

"What is happening? Are we being invaded?" I asked fearfully.

"No, that's not the sound of an invasion. This is something else." He gripped my hand and gave me a grim look. "Stay with me, Meritaten, no matter what." I nodded my promise, my eyes wide with terror. As the sounds of fear rose around us, he repeated himself as if one promise wasn't enough. "No matter what, you stay close."

With my heart pounding and my hands sweating, I let Smenkhkare drag us to our fate.

Chapter Fifteen

Bloody Sheets—Nefertiti

As soon as I left Tadukhipa's rooms, I found myself surrounded by the medjay. Their fierce tattooed eyes let me know that I faced grave danger. Horus, my husband's most trusted medjay, spoke to me directly. It was a strange thing to hear the mostly silent man's voice. "Great Queen, come with us." I didn't immediately obey him. What if they were here at the behest of one of my enemies? I had too many to count now. If the reports were true, if my husband was dead, there would be no protection for me. But how could I know if they were true? Perhaps he himself had orchestrated all this just to have a reason to seize me?

Horus spoke calmly as if he read my mind. "It is true. Your husband, our Pharaoh, is dead. Please, Great Queen. Come with us. We must keep you safe."

I held back a thousand questions and a thousand tears. This was no time to release either of those torrents. I would have to go with them now, willingly or forcibly, and what would be, would be. I nodded my permission, and immediately the medjay surrounded me. They moved in precise, synchronized lockstep, their left hands holding their spears and their right hands upon the hilts of their gleaming daggers. They banged their spear ends on the ground, and we began to walk toward whatever destination they had in mind.

If the blow is to come, let it come now!

I would not close my eyes to the danger but stared at the back of Horus' bald head as he barked orders to his men. No attack came, and I breathed a sigh of relief. I made my face a serene mask, a skill I'd learned from my time here at court, and matched their pace. We walked through the Grand Court, where many hundreds of people were already gathered. The people were looking for consolation from the royal family, some assurance that all was well. Things were most assuredly not well. Someone recognized me and began wailing, "Great Queen! Our Great Queen!"

My first instinct was to stop and comfort those who needed me, but Horus was having none of it. "No, lady. It is not safe. There is an assassin in our court. Please, there is no time."

"My children!" I exclaimed suddenly. "Bring them to me!"

"It shall be done, Great Queen." Four of the medjay broke off from the group as others surrounded me, and I watched as the dispatched men ran to various locations to find my three living children. *Please let them be alive!*

To my surprise, the medjay led me to my chambers. Horus opened the outer door and looked nervously up and down, as if he expected an army to run down the Grand Hall. Perhaps he did. "What happened, Horus? I must know!"

"An assassin murdered Pharaoh as he worshiped. He—or she—left him bleeding in the Sun Room. By the time we found him, he was dead."

"She? Has the assassin been found? Does my son know about this?"

"We are looking everywhere. We suspect Lady Ipy of involvement since her servant discovered Pharaoh's body."

I could tell by his expression that he was not telling me everything. "Please, Horus. Do not hide anything from me. If I must protect our regent, I must know what you know."

He nodded in agreement. "The lady was distraught. Pharaoh was to send her away. I can only gather she was disappointed." Horus hesitated but continued, "At one time, he intended to make her his wife. I believe that was no longer the case. She is being held in her chambers. The priests have been summoned to rule in this matter."

"What priests? Do you mean the leopard coats? Surely not, Horus! You know they have no love for us! Would you deliver us into their hands?"

In his deep voice, Horus said, "All things must be done according to the law, Great Queen. It is the priests who administer justice in such matters."

Defiance crept up my spine. "No! It is Pharaoh's regent, Smenkhkare, who must administer justice for his father! If you do as you say, you will doom us all. Is that what you want?"

"No, lady. I only seek to protect you."

"Then please, listen to me. Find Smenkhkare! Do not give the priests such authority until you have spoken to your prince. Swear it to me."

He looked unsure, but he agreed. Under no circumstance would I ever allow the priests of Amun to pass judgment on any in the royal family, not even Ipy. If she was truly guilty, she would be punished—if she had done as he suggested, I would kill her myself! But it would be a mistake to give the Amun priesthood the power of life and death over any of us. Pharaoh had taken that away from them, and now by law, the medjay would give it back?

"When you find my son, please bring him to me. I must see him."

"Yes, Great Queen."

I hurried inside to change my clothing and prepare to flee the city. Despite what I had told Horus, I would not stay here. Not for any reason! My children and I would never be safe! "Cara! Miane!" No one answered. I hurried through my living quarters and rushed into my bedchambers. Perhaps they were there. I heard the sounds of a woman crying, and it was a familiar voice—one I knew as well as my own. When I flung the doors open, I was again surprised to find that all my servants were gone, except for Menmet, who was in a crumpled pile on my bed. She was sobbing as if I had died. Perhaps she believed that I had.

"Menmet! I am here. See? I am here."

She shot up in the bed, and then I noticed she was not alone. There was another woman in my bed—and Menmet was covered in blood!

"Menmet! What has happened? Is that the assassin?" I peered through the thin veil around my bed and stumbled back in horror. My sister lay on the sheets, her face, so like my own, wearing an expression of surprise.

Menmet turned and hissed at me. With a scream, she said, "No! You are dead! I killed you! You are dead!" She glanced from me to Pah, only now realizing that she had stabbed my sister.

My head spun with grief and shock. "Lady Nephthys? Pah?" I screamed at my sister. Her mouth was slightly open, as if she had called out for help with her last breath. She was not moving, and I could see no signs of life. This could not be! She could not die like this, betrayed by my maidservant. "Move, Menmet! What have you done?"

As I stared in horror, I saw the pale sheer fabrics of my bed turn crimson. It might not be too late! The blood still flowed! I could save Pah! Then my eyes fell upon the instrument of death in Menmet's hand, a curved golden blade with a bloody edge. She rose and held her arms stiffly at her sides. Her hands were hard fists of determination and hate. She did not relinquish her blade as I instructed. Her face was a mess of makeup and blood, and she was breathing hard. I could see her skin was pale even beneath my sister's blood. "Move, Menmet. There still may be time to save her." I put my hands in front of me to calm her. She screamed, and the sound of it chilled my bones.

"You were dead. I killed you! But you are here, and I must kill you again! Why did you return? Why, lady? Must I kill you twice?"

"Menmet, grief has made you mad. Please stop what you are doing. Stop now! It is not too late, Menmet. Let me tend to my sister. Let me see her."

"Sister? Then I did not kill you?" She stared from me to Pah. "Yes, I see now. She is Nephthys! But how could you know? Nobody knew I would come here. This is your trickery at work, Desert Queen. Let that be your final thought; you killed your own sister with your trickery and deceit!"

"How long have you hated me?" I asked as I moved backward, away from the dangerous arc she made with the blade. "Why have you done this?"

"I do not hate you, Great Queen, but I will not die for you. Lady Ipy has promised me more than you ever offered. Have I not waited on you day and night, cared for you in sickness? Have I not given you everything? And you to deny me my freedom?"

"What are you talking about, Menmet? I have denied you nothing! What do you mean?"

"Lady Ipy told me what you did. How you sold me, how you intended to offer me to Pharaoh as amusement. But I won't let that happen! I won't!"

"I never did such a thing. You let Ipy poison your mind, and she has used you to kill me. You were my friend!"

"Ha! Friends, were we? When was the Great Queen of Egypt ever my friend? My father is right—you are the poison in the ka of Egypt! We must purge our souls if we want to be reunited with Amun! Lady Ipy has done her part, and now I must do mine!"

I saw Pah move on the bed behind Menmet. Her fingers only, but she moved! I had to draw the deranged girl's attention away and get help. "Move, Menmet. Move now! I will forgive you if you move. I will help you!"

She answered with a yelp and charged at me. As she came toward me, her knife raised high, she swung again and again. I dodged the first two attempts, but then I fell on my back, and she struck my arm. It was only a glancing strike, but she left a gash on my forearm. Blood poured down my arm as we wrestled together.

I continued to scream, "Menmet! No!" but it did little good. She gritted her teeth in anger and struggled with me as if she did mean to take my life—again!

"You should have died the first time, Great Queen!"

"Menmet!" Another voice echoed through the chamber as my son drew his blade and rushed toward me. Meritaten screamed in surprise as she entered the room, but Menmet didn't seem to hear them, so focused was she on her murderous deed.

"Menmet, stop!" I screamed at her when I saw that Smenkhkare had unsheathed his blade. He drove it through her tiny body, and she lurched beneath his blow. Blood surged from her mouth, and I felt her urinate on me as the curved blade fell out of her hand. She toppled to the right, and her wig covered her face. I could not see if she was alive or dead. I did not care. I crawled to the bed and leaned over Pah.

"Pah! Pah! Quickly, Meritaten, call for the physician!" My daughter flew out of the room as Smenkhkare examined Menmet. "Please, sister, look at me!"

She had little life left in her. How could she live with all the blood she'd lost? I was not proficient in the healing arts, but even I knew this. "Pah, don't leave me."

Her brow furrowed slightly and her mouth moved, but no words came forth.

I leaned closer. "What is it? My sister, please don't leave me."

"Nef-ret...for-give..."

I sobbed and held her cool hand. I kissed it and nodded. "Yes, I forgive you. Forgive *me*, Pah. Please don't leave me."

"A life...for..."

And then she was gone. Pah's eyes closed, her breathing ceased, and her face went slack. It was peaceful, as if she knew that at last, she would have peace.

Meritaten was not gone long. "Mother, the physician cannot be found. The palace is in turmoil...and the medjay. They are gone!" Meritaten touched my shoulder as I wept. Her words snatched me from my grief. I could not allow my treasures to perish under the blades of the priests. With clumsy fingers, I took Pah's bracelet. I had to have something of hers.

"We must go! Where is Tasherit?"

"I know where she is. She is safe in Princess Sitamen's aviary, but how will we get there without being seen? Will the priests kill us, Mother? Did the priests kill Father?"

"Never doubt their hand was in it, no matter who drew the blade, Meritaten. I have made arrangements for us to leave since I feared this day would come." I glanced at Pah one last time. "We must get Tasherit and leave, for the city is lost to us."

"No!" Smenkhkare shouted in anger. "I am the Pharaoh of Egypt. I will not flee like a child in the night. I will fight for what is mine."

"You might fight, but you will lose. Come with us, Smenkhkare. It is the only way. There will be another day for fighting."

He stepped back and shoved his sword back in his sheath. "No, you must go. I will take my throne. And when I do, I will send for you."

"No!" Meritaten yelled at him through her tears. "You promised we would always be together. You cannot leave me, brother. You cannot!"

He held her by the shoulders and spoke to her in low tones, "Please listen to me. You must take care of Mother and Tasherit, but I have many others I have to care for. Do you think I can leave Egypt, our Egypt, in the hands of the priests of Amun? I cannot do such a thing. Father has trusted me with this, and I will not fail him. Now go. I will send for you."

As Smenkhkare kissed her, I ransacked my dresser, pulled out a few private treasures, and stuck them in a bag. I hid the bag in my skirts and took Meritaten by the arm.

"Come, show me where your sister is," I said. Smenkhkare left us, and Meritaten called after him. He did not return. "Please, Meritaten," I continued. "Show me where. Where have you hidden her?"

"I told you, she is in Sitamen's aviary."

Without a word, I grasped her hand, and together we fled down the Great Hall. I feared greatly that someone would see us and seize us, but no one did. As we traveled through the corridors, I saw heartrending displays of greed. The people were looting the court! But then the medjay appeared, and with them a battalion of armed priests. "No! Meritaten! We must go through the tunnels."

We ran through the Bull Room, and I slapped the trigger wall to open the door. Then we slipped through the small entranceway. It was dark inside, so dark I could barely see my hand in front of my face. Meritaten tripped over her own feet and whimpered in the dark, but still I pulled us toward the aviary. At least, I thought it was the aviary. Where was I? A light shone in the distance, and I didn't know whether to run toward it or away from it. I was thankful my sometimes-wise husband had built these tunnels into his palace. Perhaps he knew all along this day would come. I never would have dreamed that one day all of Egypt would turn on us, especially not my dear Menmet!

"Mother, this way!" Smenkhkare! I ran toward him. "I couldn't abandon you. The palace is too full of priests. I have hidden Tasherit there!"

I saw the lid of a large clay pot lift, and my daughter's head poked out. She cried when she saw me.

"My treasure!" I lifted her from the jar and kissed her cheek.

"Quickly! They are coming now! I can see them in the distance. Where do we go, Mother?"

Please, Amenhotep! Help me!

I heard a scraping sound to my left. Someone had opened a nearby wall. There were many entrances into our secret tunnels, and unfortunately, someone had discovered one very nearby.

Go to the right, to the wall that leads to the Crescent Pool. And then on to the Green Temple.

Adijah would meet us there, or so we had arranged. But what if he betrayed me, as Menmet had? Then let me first die! I pushed ahead of them. "Take your sister's hand, Meritaten. Follow me!"

I raced down the narrow corridor. The voices of the intruders now bounced off the stone walls, and they were getting closer. I glanced back to see my son turn with his weapon drawn. "No! Run, Smenkhkare! Run!" Thankfully he listened and we surged forward, Tasherit crying while Meritaten prayed. I could hear the running of the water; the Crescent Pool was near here. "Wave your torch this way!" With one flick of his torch, I could see the brass handle on the wall. I pulled it, and my children and I ran out of the hall. Smenkhkare attempted to push the door back, but I warned him, "It won't move. It is set on a sand timer. Come now!" We ran to the small gate, which was a minor entrance, one used by the gardeners who stocked the pool and cared for Pharaoh's private sanctuary. The guards must have overlooked or forgotten it. We ran through the shadowy arbors and out the open gate. *Thank you, Amenhotep!*

When we got to the streets, there was chaos. Fires were burning, and the leopard coats moved quickly to rid the city of heretics. Any Egyptians who were faithful to Amenhotep and Nefertiti were the first to be dispatched. I recognized some, but there was nothing I could do for them. There was no trial for these innocents. They were guilty of believing in Amenhotep's vision. Guilty of abandoning the Amun temples. They were delivered a speedy death on sight.

I wept against the wall but did not allow myself the luxury of grief for long. "We must go to the Green Temple. A friend waits there for us."

Smenkhkare took in the sight of the murders, and I saw his jaw set, just as his father's had done when he was overcome with anger. I touched his arm, and together we journeyed to the Green Temple. Smenkhkare came across an abandoned wagon and, searching through it, found and tossed us all some clothing. "Cover up. The closer we get to the Temple of Isis, the greater the chance that someone will recognize you. Leave your robes and wig here, Mother. Here, put this on."

Taking the bundle of rough fabric he handed me, I did as he asked. Smenkhkare also shed his headdress and put on a plain brown robe. He tossed his gold prince's cuffs in the wagon as payment for our robbery. His eyes widened to see my shaved head, but he said nothing. There was no time for such questions.

"Tasherit, Mother will carry you. Mother, Meritaten, keep your faces covered."

We scurried down the colonnade that led to the front gates of the temple. We were too late. The priests of Amun were here and were attempting to enter that holy place. I gasped at the sheer number of them.

As if she read my mind, Meritaten whispered, "There must be hundreds. They will kill us!"

"Nefertiti," a voice whispered. A hooded figure stood at the end of the nearby alleyway. He pushed back his hood, and I could plainly see Adijah's fair hair. He waved, and I began to run toward him.

Tasherit whimpered, and I shushed her. "Keep quiet, Tasherit. We will be safe soon. All will be well."

"Yes, Mother," she whispered into my clothing.

We made it to the Grecian warrior, and I struggled for breath. I had not run so far in a long time. My lungs were burning, my feet ached, and my arms hurt, but I would not put my daughter down. "This way. There is a wagon that will get us out of town. We must go to the hills for now. We will hide until the priests stop looking and then go across the sea. I have everything ready, as I promised your sister I would. Here, let me hold her." I handed Tasherit to Adijah and reached behind me for Meritaten, but she was gone. As I looked down the alley, I could see Smenkhkare and Meritaten running hand in hand back to the city.

"No!" I screamed in anger. I tried to run after them, but Adijah prevented me.

"You cannot help them. If we go back into the city, you will die. They have made their choice, lady. We must go."

"I cannot leave my treasures," I said in tears. "What will become of them?"

Adijah did not scold me. He simply asked, "And what about this one?" Tasherit was sobbing for her sister.

He was right. There was nothing to be done. I had to leave Meritaten and Smenkhkare to their own fate. What was done was done. Could I allow Pah's sacrifice to be in vain? She had saved me, and she had saved Tasherit.

"Very well. Let's go." With tears streaming down my face, I left Amarna behind. Never again would we see the glory of Egypt. Never again would I behold the face of my son, the face so like my husband's. Sweet, loving Meritaten would always be absent from my arms.

Farewell, Amenhotep. You will remain in my dreams.

Epilogue

New Treasures—Tasherit

"Come, let me hold you, my own dear treasure." Mother's aged hands reached for me, and I did not hesitate to put my hands in hers. She was not prone to show affection, at least not as she once had. I'd learned to accept it when it was offered, for I loved her with all my being. I pretended I did not notice how twisted and old her hands looked. I winced at seeing the scars again, painful reminders of the sacrifice she'd made that last night in Amarna. I had similar burns on my legs, but they were not as severe as hers. The flames had licked me, but I had healed. Her skin had been forever changed by the conflagration. The once-proud queen had taken great pains in recent years to keep her hands covered in her robes when they weren't occupied with whatever task she was working on. Most days, that was drying fish or selling ribbons to the visitors who came to our island for its healing waters.

Adijah had abandoned his sword long ago and traded it for a boat. That had been our life since our escape from Egypt. After months of grieving and mourning for my siblings, Mother had come around again, ready to face life and whatever challenges it might offer. And she was finally mine exclusively, except for her nights, which she spent with Adijah. But that was all coming to an end now. She would be gone soon.

I had seen myself grieve, and now I must live that grief. And with her passing would pass the last of my family.

"Oh, my Meritaten. I have missed you."

I sighed as she enveloped me in her bony arms. It would do no good to correct her. She would be dead before the sun rose. Yes, I had seen it in the fire and the water many months ago. Until her sickness last moon, I had no reason to expect her death. From my first memory until that moment, my mother had always been a vital woman, full of energy and focused on whatever purpose she put her mind to.

Although the memories of the painted walls of Egypt had faded to muted scenes from another life, tonight they were all around us, at least in our spirits. I could almost see my favorite panel shimmering behind her, as it had when I visited her apartments in the Great Palace. There was no lack of colorful things to see in Amenhotep's city, but this particular scene had enchanted me no end. Besides the broad swath of blue water that represented the Nile, there were many boats and fishermen. But best of all, there were hundreds of animals. I recognized the cruel crocodile and the spindly storks, but there were also strange fishes, half-fish and half-human creatures, and so many animals I had never seen before, and that was saying something. As the children of Pharaoh, we were often gifted with queer little animals and playful birds, and even fish in colorful bowls.

During those visits to Mother's apartments, I would quiz my sister until she grew bored, and then Mother would invite me into her lap. She would repeat the names to me and tell me stories about them. And such stories she told! Mother had a way of making everything seem magical.

Perhaps it had been a silly goal, a child's dream, but how I wanted to see the river before I died! I could not understand why no one would take me. It wasn't that far. However, during every Sed and Sokar Festival and on every journey to the Island Temple, I was left behind with a promise that next year, I would be permitted to attend.

But I never saw the blue waters of the Nile. I ached for the river. I longed for it as if it were a part of me. A part I would never know.

"Mother, tell me about the river." I leaned against her and let her stroke my hair. It was no matter that my hair was as white as hers. It was no matter that I had children of my own. No, I now had grandchildren. None of that mattered. For a few minutes, she was the Great Queen Nefertiti still, and I was her beloved daughter, Tasherit. I closed my eyes and waited to hear her tell me the story of the river and all the animals that called it home.

"What shall I tell you, Tasherit? Surely you recall all their names by now."

My heart fluttered to hear her call me by my name, my true name! No one called me by my royal name anymore. Not even my husband, Herxes. Here on the small island of Cythera, we were not to mention the past. Even now, I could see Adijah's disapproving look at the mention of my former name. But what could it matter now? Egypt's evil priests did not search for us any longer, if they ever had. They had peaked in power. I prayed that somehow they would be called to account for the blood they had shed. No, Adijah did not frighten me, and I knew he would deny my mother nothing. He loved her more than she loved him, but he was not unhappy with that arrangement. To the once-mighty warrior, she was always the Great Queen of Egypt, even if he did not want anyone to know his wife's true identity. He always treated her with great deference and honor.

"Tell me, Great Queen, my mother. Tell me about them."

"Let us look, then, Dearest One. See there? There floats the mighty Zephonites, the strongest crocodile in the river. He is very old, so old that he takes very long naps, sometimes for months, before he reappears to fill his belly with fish or whatever else he finds. And that in the corner there is the Hydrus! No animal can defeat Zephonites but Hydrus. Ah, he is clever. He allows himself to be eaten, and when the King of the Crocodiles thinks he's won, the Hydrus bursts out of his belly and kills the monster."

I did not shiver as I once had when she told me such tales, but I loved hearing again the tale of the Eternal Battle. She was skipping many details, but she was tired. I knew she was tired. I would not correct her or ask her excited questions to dig for more information as I had when I was a child.

Thinking to redirect her mind from the monstrous creatures and thoughts of death and destruction, I asked, "What of the Singers, Mother? Tell me about them."

She did not answer me immediately but clutched me to her as she coughed and struggled to claim another gasp of air. Her breathing sounded shallow, and I could hear the rattling of her lungs, but I could not let her go. I would not. I wanted to keep her talking. If she was talking, she was living. It was selfish, but I couldn't let her leave me. Adijah offered her a cup of water, but she shook her head. I closed my eyes and clung to Mother as if I might go with her when she died if I were quiet and still.

Yes, perhaps I could fool death. Maybe Osiris would take me too. He hung in the sky tonight...maybe he would!

"The Singers now appear as frogs, croakers large and small, but they were once beautiful women who gathered at the river and sang to Osiris every night. They hoped to seduce the god and have children by him, but Isis intervened and transformed the sisters into green frogs. Osiris had pity on them, and although he could not change them back, he did grant them their wish. He entered the water and cast his seed upon them. And now as frogs, they continue to reproduce, and they sing there still."

I said suddenly, "Mother, do not leave me. How can I live without you?"

"Oh, my own daughter. You are stronger than you know. You are brave and have treasures of your own now. And I promise you, we will see one another again. All will be well."

A moan caught in my throat. "How can you know that, Mother? How can you possibly know that? And I am not strong, not at all."

She kissed my head and said quietly, "Hush now, Tasherit. I know because I have seen it in the fire and the water, the same as you."

"But I have not seen that, Mother. How I want to see that! Show me, please."

She coughed and patted my shoulder. "Yes, I will show you. Stir up the fire, daughter. Stir it up, and we will look together."

I didn't want to move from her arms, but how could I deny her? I had asked for this, hadn't I? I left her arms, tossed a twisted grass log onto the fire and watched it smoke. There were few trees here, but the grass logs burned long and hot. I tried not to spy on Adijah as he came to her, whispered in her ear, kissed her, and quickly departed. Even after all these years, it seemed strange that Mother would kiss anyone but Father. She'd been so devoted to him, as we all had until he cast us off. Her love for Adijah was not white-hot and long-suffering as it had been with the Pharaoh of Egypt, but it seemed to make her happy. He glanced at me sadly as he left us alone. As always, the warrior was uncomfortable with our magic. He did not believe in such things, but neither did he speak against it.

"What do you see, Tasherit?" She leaned back against her pillow and closed her eyes.

I squatted and poked at the firepot. "Nothing yet, Mother. I look still." And I did. There was nothing in the flames, only color and sparks.

"Keep looking. You will see. Soon you will see."

I reached behind me and squeezed her hand briefly, but I kept my eyes on the fire. I wanted to see. I *had* to see. I needed to know! Would I see her again? And what about Smenkhkare and Meritaten? We knew about their horrible deaths; they had ruled for less than two years before they too were murdered. Smenkhkare never sent for us. They had traveled to the Otherworld together, and together they would always be, as they wanted. But what of my glorious father and my aunt Nephthys? I stared hard and began to see the shifting in the center of the flames.

"I see a figure, Mother! Something is moving in the flames!"

She coughed again, but I kept my focus. "Keep looking, Meritaten." *Oh, no,* I thought. *Her mind is wandering again.* She would soon forget my name forever. *Please, let me see before she leaves me and forgets me.*

The flames shimmered, just as they always did when magic moved in them. I gasped as the image cleared. I could plainly see the painted wall! "Mother!" I exclaimed at the sight.

"Keep looking," she whispered assuredly.

I saw my sister's round face, and my hand flew to my mouth in surprise. Never before had I seen the dead in the fire or the water. I laughed with joy. "Meritaten!" I pointed at her excitedly. Suddenly, standing beside her was our brother Smenkhkare. He looked handsome, his royal garments clean and white, as they always were in life. His arm went protectively around Meritaten's waist. I saw no horrific wounds, no bloody gashes; whatever they had suffered through was no more. Death was not as I had imagined. No, here they were alive and together somehow.

Then there were other familiar faces. Some I knew by name, others I did not, but they knew me. I could see by their expressions that they knew I watched them through the flames. My eyes burned and my throat felt raw from the heat, but I would not relent. I called to them, but they did not speak to me. They spoke only to each other, but they were happy to see me. This I knew. Then they faded, and my father appeared. His hands were on the shoulders of my brothers—and yes, there was my little sister. She had died when she was just a babe, but she was a babe no more. How did I know she was my sister? She looked so much like me, like my father.

"Mother, I see them. I see them all!" I cried with joy to see them, and then I felt the air shift and change. The warmth of the fire faded, although the flames continued to flutter. The cold was so deep it hurt my bones, but it passed over me quickly, and the warmth returned. I heard a sigh behind me, but I could not bear to look away from the scene before me.

And then I saw her in the flames.

There was Mother's face, young and beautiful. Long red hair flowing, green eyes playful and happy. She wore no makeup, no heavy eye paint, as used to be her custom. Yes, she wore the prettiest smile I'd ever seen on her pink lips. It was as if she were young again. Father held his arms out to her, and she fell into them. They embraced one another as if all was forgotten, all was forgiven. I sobbed to see their reconciliation. Then I felt a great sadness because they had forgotten me. Or so I thought, until I remembered her words.

Tasherit...you will see...

Unexpectedly the flame died, and with it the images. Despite my desperate attempts to revive the fire, I could not call them back. I would never be able to see them like this again, for with her passing, my magic left me. I would learn this later.

I turned to see what I already knew. My mother, the Great Queen of Egypt, had left this world for the next. It had not been a vain seeing. I had seen her. There would be no fine funeral for her. No sacrifices made, no hidden tombs or mystical prayers. She had been here, and now she was gone.

But I had peace now. Heavy grief, but peace came too. I *would* see her again. I would see them all one day. Until then, I would tell everyone who would listen the story of the Desert Queen. She had been the Falcon of the Meshwesh, the mekhma of the Red Lands. The Beloved Queen of Amenhotep, Neferneferuaten.

Yes, I would be the one to make sure everyone knew the truth, despite what Adijah said. What was there to fear now? I arranged Mother's body on the pallet, gently placed her arms at her sides, and smoothed her long hair over her shoulders. I tidied her gown and covered her hands as she always liked.

Tonight, all the people of Cythera and the surrounding islands would come to honor her. And after they said their words and cast gifts upon her, I would tell them a story. I knew what I would say.

Come closer, my Treasures. Let me tell you the Tale of Nefret.

Connect with M.L. Bullock on Facebook[1]. To receive updates on her latest releases, visit her website at M.L. Bullock[2] and subscribe to her mailing list. You can also contact her at authormlbullock@gmail.com.

About the Author

Author of the best-selling *Seven Sisters* series and the *Gulf Coast Paranormal* series, M.L. Bullock has been storytelling since she was a child. A student of archaeology, she loves weaving stories that feature her favorite historical characters—including Nefertiti. She currently lives on the Gulf Coast with her family but travels frequently to explore the southern states she loves so much.

---

1.   https://www.facebook.com/AuthorMLBullock

2.   http://www.mlbullock.com

Don't miss out!

Visit the website below and you can sign up to receive emails whenever M.L. Bullock publishes a new book. There's no charge and no obligation.

https://books2read.com/r/B-A-CXMC-PZHMB

BOOKS 2 READ

Connecting independent readers to independent writers.

Also by M.L. Bullock

Desert Queen Saga
The Tale of Nefret
The Falcon Rises
The Kingdom of Nefertiti
The Song of the Bee Eater

Gulf Coast Paranormal Trilogy Series
Ghosted
Haunted
Dead
Spooked
Paranormal

Haunting Passions
Her Haunted Heart

Scary Fall Stories
Horrible Little Things

Seven Sisters
Seven Sisters
Ghost on a Swing

Twelve to Midnight
Mary Twelves
Pieces of Twelves

Standalone
Christmas at Seven Sisters
Delivered Me From Evil

Watch for more at www.mlbullock.com.

About the Author

Author M.L. Bullock enjoys the laid-back atmosphere and the spooky vibe of the Gulf Coast, especially the region's historic districts and sites. When she isn't visiting her favorite haunts in New Orleans or Old Mobile, you can find her flipping through old photographs or newspaper clippings in search of new inspiration.

Read more at www.mlbullock.com.

www.ingramcontent.com/pod-product-compliance
Lightning Source LLC
Chambersburg PA
CBHW071203130726
47998CB00002B/595